The Coffee House Sleuths

Sleighed

The Coffee House Sleuths

Sleighed

Book 1

T. LOCKHAVEN

EDITED BY:
EMMY ELLIS
GRACE LOCKHAVEN

TWISTED KEY
publishing

2019

First Printing: 2019

ISBN 978-1-947744-41-7

Twisted Key Publishing, LLC
www.twistedkeypublishing.com

Ordering Information:
Special discounts are available on quantity purchases by corporations, associations, educators, and others. For details, contact the publisher at the above listed address.

U.S. trade bookstores and wholesalers: Please contact Twisted Key Publishing, LLC by email twistedkeypublishing@gmail.com.

Contents

Chapter 1 1

Chapter 2 12

Chapter 3 33

Chapter 4 40

Chapter 5 49

Chapter 6 61

Chapter 7 75

Chapter 8 97

Chapter 9 107

Chapter 10 113

Chapter 11 132

Chapter 1

"What's a party without mistletoe?" Michael asked, arching his eyebrows. He took a sip of pumpkin spice coffee and gazed expectantly at his two best friends.

Ellie and Olivia shared a look that could only be interpreted as: *Not this again.*

"I see," Michael deduced, "the silent treatment. When it came to discussing whether our Christmas tree lights should flicker, you couldn't stop talking. But, I suggest a pristine piece of nature that just happens to be intertwined with a time-honored tradition, and suddenly you have nothing to say."

Ellie took a sip of coffee and checked her watch.

Olivia licked creamy parfait from her spoon. "I love this song." She smiled. *"Silent Night*, how poignant."

Michael leaned in, his blue eyes sparkling mischievously. "Mistletoe has virtually ruined people's lives. We have the ability to unleash—"

"Here we go," Ellie complained.

"It's funny, one little sprig hung over a doorway induces equal amounts of annoyance and awkwardness. It's the epitome of...well, it's just funny." He sat back in his chair and clasped his hands.

"Are you done bloviating?" Ellie asked.

Michael glanced at her, held up a finger, and then wrinkled his forehead. "I'm not sure, I'll need to consult with my thesaurus before answering that—or my lawyer," he added.

"Mistletoe is not funny, Michael West," Olivia blurted out, brandishing her well-licked spoon in his direction.

Ellie put her hand on Olivia's. "Don't, darling, stay strong."

Olivia scanned the café, tightened her lips, and then leaned in, whispering furiously, "Do you remember Mary Stewart?"

"That sweet old lady? Wasn't she the church secretary at Sacred Heart?" Ellie asked, gently blowing across her coffee.

"Yes, well, a branch of mistletoe made her pee behind the bushes at the Weston Country Club...."

"Well, you're not supposed to eat it," Michael exclaimed. "She's lucky she didn't die."

"Shh," Olivia hushed Michael, pointing at him. "She didn't eat it, you moron. Father McKenzie thought it would be funny to hang a branch of mistletoe at the entrance to the bathrooms." She took in a deep breath, recalling the memory. "He just stood there, a twisted smile on his face...waiting with his wintergreen Tic-Tacs. I can still hear the *tap-tap, tap-tap*, as he shook them into his hand...loitering for his next victim."

"Okay." Michael nodded. "That took a much darker turn than I expected."

"I remember Father McKenzie said something horrible like, 'Before you pee, you gotta kiss me.'"

"Ugh." Ellie visibly shuddered. "That's disgusting. He has old man lips."

"Okay…." Michael held out his hands. "First, you guys have completely deviated from what I was talking about. Secondly, you basically vilified mistletoe by adding a sinister component. How much do you want to bet I can prove mistletoe is conditional?"

Ellie looked at Olivia and shrugged. "Sure, dazzle us with your intellect."

"Thank you. In the spirit of fairness, what if I replaced Father McKenzie with someone like Chris Hemsworth or Ewan McGregor in this scenario. I'm sure things would be much different. You see? …Conditional…."

"Totally different," Ellie insisted. "You can't take a hypothetical and try to merge it with reality. This whole discussion is ridiculous. I mean, really, Michael, if you're so desperate for a kiss from a woman, man up and ask for it."

"Wait! Wait, I wasn't saying that, I can get a kiss! I simply wanted to watch—"

"Michael West, that is much more disturbing on many levels," Olivia muttered.

"You didn't let me finish, that was completely out of context—"

"Listen," Ellie interrupted, "I need to make a point, and after this," she insisted, turning to each of her friends, "we are *through* discussing mistletoe, agreed? We *are* adults after all."

Olivia and Michael nodded in unison.

"At least two of us," Olivia sighed under her breath.

"I believe that the mistletoe tradition was created by a sad, sad man named either Lester or Morris," Ellie began. "I'm going to go with Lester—an aficionado of skintight, forest-green, mock-turtleneck sweaters, pleated khakis accessorized with a reversible belt, argyle socks, and white patent-leather shoes with tassels."

"Make sure you breathe, Ellie," Michael interjected.

Ellie narrowed her eyes. "And before I slam my gavel down to end this inane discussion, I would like to add that it's a pitifully sad, outdated tradition for lonely men who enjoy puzzles, the game Magic, and celibacy."

"Hear! Hear! Well done, you," Olivia declared and pounded her fist on the table. "Well done."

"Indeed," Michael said, scooting his chair outside of Ellie's arm reach, "but just for clarity, for our holiday party, mistletoe in, or out? I'm asking for a friend."

Michael was saved from almost certain death when a man's voice erupted from the table behind them, cutting through the conversational noise at the Bitter Sweet Café.

"Turn up the volume on the television," was directed at the thirty-something hipster running the cash register.

Ellie and Olivia twisted in their seats to see what the commotion was about.

The local news was showing video footage, obviously shot from someone's cell phone. The crawler at the bottom of the screen read: *Lana Cove Mall Mayhem*.

"Oh no." Michael sucked in his breath, frightened there had been a shooting.

From the expressions on Olivia's and Ellie's faces, they were thinking the same thing.

The video panned from the floor to Santa, seated on a large golden chair with red plush upholstery. Standing to his side was an angelic elf with blonde hair, a green top, red-and-white-striped stockings, and pointy green shoes. A long line of children queued in front of Santa, waiting for their turn.

The videographer was obviously enamored with the elf, because the camera zoomed in and remained there for some time. It wasn't until she turned with a surprised expression, that the video swooped from her to another man dressed as Santa leaping out from behind the other Santa's chair.

The entire café gasped when the rogue Santa ripped the beard off the seated Santa's face. Then, as if it were a trophy, he thrust the beard into the air and screamed, "He's a fake! He's a fake!"

For a second, the de-bearded Santa didn't seem to know what to do. He glanced around, bewildered. Then he jumped to his feet and chased the other Santa around the stage. The children scattered, screaming.

The rogue Santa, still clutching the fake beard, crashed through a candy cane barrier and sprinted toward the escalator.

"Is that George?" Ellie asked, horrified. "Please tell me that's not George."

"I'm not sure," Michael said, unable to tear his eyes from the train wreck.

The beardless Santa dove for the rogue, grabbing him by the back of his pants, just as he'd stepped onto the escalator. As fate would have it, Santa's pants dropped to his boots, revealing a pair of silk boxers tastefully decorated with candy canes.

"Thank God for that," Michael said. "It could have been worse—a lot worse."

The rogue waddled and fell forward onto the escalator. Beardless Santa leaped onto his back. Horrified onlookers gawked and pointed as the literal Santa sandwich slowly ascended, still fighting over the beard.

The news anchor appeared on the screen, a headshot of the rogue behind her shoulder. "It saddens me to say," the woman said in a crisp voice, "a spokesman from the Lana Cove Mall tells us that

George Owens will be banned from the mall until further notice."

The atmosphere inside the Bitter Sweet Café immediately shifted from festive to dismay. Whispered conversations filled the room. For many, George was a close, dear friend.

"I don't understand.... Why would he do that?" Ellie asked, her heart breaking for George.

"He wouldn't," Olivia insisted. "This doesn't make any sense."

"Honestly," Michael replied, "he looked like a man pushed to his limits."

"Livs and I have known George for over thirty years. He's never been in trouble, he's just a sweet old man."

"And who was that other Santa?" Michael asked. "Did either of you recognize him?"

"I don't know," Ellie said, thinking. "I don't think I've ever seen him before. George has been the official Santa at the Lana Cove Mall since before I was born."

"I can't imagine." Olivia frowned. "Why do they have to keep showing that video over and over again? It's like they revel in other people's misery."

"Daryl," Ellie called out to the hipster employee. "Change the channel. Put on anything, I don't care if it's golf."

"I hear George has been tipping it back a little too much lately," a man said a couple tables away.

"Great." Ellie nodded toward the man. "That's how rumors get started. Do you think we should reach out to George and make sure he's okay? He's bound to be devastated."

"Maybe we could invite him to our Christmas party," Olivia offered. "We could use a real Santa. No offense, Michael, you do make a great Santa."

"None taken. I'm always willing to do what needs to be done for the greater good. Besides, I'm dying to try on my new holiday threads, so it's a win-win."

"Actually, I'm pretty sure George is booked up by now," Ellie replied. "He's usually busy from the beginning of December through Christmas."

"I wouldn't be too sure about that." Michael stared at the television. "Take it from someone who's done digital marketing his entire life…this is the type of story that goes viral. Trust me." He shook his head. "There's not a lot of people who are going to want an unhinged Santa."

"I agree." Ellie sighed. "I think we should invite him to the party. If he has a Santa gig, well, that's great, but if not, I'm sure he could use the support of his friends right now."

Chapter 2

Michael turned his face toward the sky and closed his eyes. Snowflakes fell lazily onto his cheeks, like tiny cold kisses. For a moment, he was back in Boston, his daughter's delicate mittened hand in his, running through the snow, seeing who could catch a snowflake on their tongue—memories of Lexis dragging him to the ground to make snow angels. His heart soared at the sound of her laughter, and for that fleeting moment in time, everything was simple, everything was perfect in the world.

The sound of a car passing brought him back to the present.

He breathed in deeply. His daughter, now eighteen, was away in France this year, traveling with her best friend's family for Christmas. This would be his first Christmas without her since his divorce and his new life in Lana Cove. A tear trekked slowly down his face. He stuck out his tongue, catching a snowflake. It melted, just like his heart.

A gentle *tap, tap* caught his attention. He glanced toward his house. Ellie stood at the picture window, her face aglow, lit from the candles she placed on the ledge. Michael waved and turned away, embarrassed to be caught in such a private moment.

He'd used the excuse of shoveling the sidewalk to go outside and be alone with his thoughts, but the truth was, it wasn't necessary. A thin dusting of snow that reminded him of powdered sugar was all that blanketed the walkway and the porch. And with a few whisks from his push broom, he'd cleared the pavement and the porch.

"All right, Michael," he whispered, "get ahold of yourself." He clomped up the porch steps, leaned the broom against the house, kicked the snow off his boots, and stepped inside.

"Welcome back." Ellie smiled. "Beautiful, isn't it?" Her face was pressed to the window, her hands on either side of her head.

"It is," Michael said, talking about Ellie, just as much as he was the snow.

He removed his jacket and scarf and hung them in the closet, and then with the grace of an Olympic skater, he slid sock-footed across the floor and grabbed Ellie's hand. Drawing her in close, he slow danced with her. He spun her like a ballerina and pulled her in. She leaned her head on his shoulder for a moment, her dark silken hair spilling across his chest, then she turned her head and looked into his eyes.

"Michael," she whispered softly, her eyes wide, filled with wonderment.

His heart jumped. "Yes?" He was intoxicated by her beauty.

"The Christmas tree isn't going to make itself." She smiled, playfully pushing him away.

Michael's heart skipped a beat, and his brain had gone to mush. "Wait, what did you say?" This didn't feel at all like the magical moment he'd just envisioned in his mind.

"I said the Christmas tree needs to be set up."

"You ruin a beautiful moment because of a tree?"

"Beautiful moment? All I see is an empty corner, and not a lot of time before our guests arrive. Tick-tock," Ellie prompted, tapping an imaginary watch.

"How long could it possibly take to put up a Christmas tree?"

"I'll take this question." Olivia walked into the room with three glasses of wine. She handed a glass each to Ellie and Michael. "Do you remember last year?"

"Which part?" Michael asked curiously. "I already apologized for saying your dad looked like a tall Napoleon. I believe I even used the word doppelganger to impress him."

Ellie gave him a you're-walking-on-thin-ice glare.

"What?" Michael defended himself. "He always had his arm across his chest, with his hand hidden, just like Napoleon."

"His arm was in a sling, you idiot," Olivia retorted. "Remember he shattered it trying to teach you how to water ski?"

"Oh yeah, I remember some of that," Michael replied sheepishly. "So wait, you're still angry about that?"

"No! We're talking about the Christmas tree. I was asking if you remembered last year and what happened regarding your assembly of the tree."

"Hmm." Michael tapped his finger on his chin. "Not really. I seem to remember something about you constantly asking us to test the punch, test the eggnog…and after that it gets a little hazy. I feel like you may have taken advantage of me."

"Hah, don't flatter yourself. Let's just say we found you asleep on the floor, curled around the base of a half-finished tree."

"Oh yeah…," Michael nodded. "I recall some pictures on Facebook. I was wrapped up in silver tinsel with a star attached to my head."

"Good times." Olivia laughed.

"Tell you what," Ellie said, "why don't you set up the tables and put out the dishes. Olivia and I will assemble this beautiful plastic Douglas fir."

"Are you sure?" Michael shrugged. "I mean, aren't men better at assembling things like furniture? Something about spatial awareness."

Ellie narrowed her eyes. "Michael, we're going to pretend like you didn't just say that, and maybe, we'll let you live."

Michael opened his mouth to object but decided against it. "Got it," he mumbled. "Table, dishes, silverware, DJ."

"What was that last part?" Ellie demanded.

"Nothing," Michael called back. He patted his iPhone and smiled, disappearing into the kitchen.

🌲🌲🌲🌲

"Ellie, you've checked the clock a dozen times. He'll be here."

"I'm worried about him." Ellie stared out the window. "The party starts in thirty minutes, and I really want to talk with George before the guests arrive."

"I'm sure he'll—" Olivia nearly jumped out of her skin when the doorbell rang. "That's probably him now."

Ellie rushed across the room and threw open the door. "George!" She beamed.

"Hi, Ellie." George smiled kindly, brushing the snow from his coat and hat. His eyes appeared tired and sad, his large, bulbous nose and cheeks red from the cold.

"Come in, come in," Ellie gushed. "Did you walk here?" She leaned through the doorway, peering outside for George's bright-red Chrysler Lebaron with wood paneling, made to resemble Santa's sled. "Where's your car? I would have certainly—" She caught herself. "I'm sorry, George, too many questions."

"It's okay, Ellie, I understand."

She moved to the side to give him room. He stomped his boots on the welcome mat and then stepped inside.

She stared at him. *If anyone looks like Santa, it's George.*

"The decorations are beautiful." His voice sounded rough and weary. "You've outdone yourself."

"The decorations are Olivia's handiwork. She's unbelievably talented."

"Hi, George!" Olivia chirped. She wrapped her arms around him. "It's so good to see you. Can I get you a coffee? Punch? Eggnog?"

"Coffee would be nice, thank you, Olivia."

"You got it. I'll add a dash of cinnamon to spice things up a bit." She winked.

Michael appeared in the living room in a pink apron with red piping, the word Sweet-buns elegantly embroidered across the front. He followed George's eyes from his face, down to his apron. "It was a gift," he offered. "And," he said defensively, "it's the truth."

George shook his head and laughed. "Does it come with matching slippers?"

"No, but in case I don't get a chance to come sit on your lap, you'll know what I want for Christmas," Michael teased. "George," he nodded, "it's always good to see you. I've been banished to the kitchen, so I'm gonna get back to my balls."

Ellie turned to George and shook her head as Michael headed back to the kitchen. "I'm not sure if he sets himself up like that on purpose or if he's really that naïve."

"Sausage balls," Michael yelled from the kitchen. "Get your minds out of the gutter."

"Perhaps it's a little of both," George suggested playfully. He paused and inhaled. "Thank you for inviting me."

"George," she asked delicately, "are you doing okay? We saw that God-awful video on the news, and you've been on our minds ever since."

"I'm all right. Well, I'm not all right, I guess I just feel—"

"Unwanted?" Michael suggested, returning to the room with a pan of sizzling sausage balls.

Ellie gave Michael a what-is-your-problem look and smacked him on the back of the head.

"Sorry," he muttered.

"Well, I was going for betrayed." George's voice caught in his throat. "But I guess unwanted would fit in there just as well, too."

"See?" Michael gestured with a spatula, "He said *unwanted*, so, we're all on the same page."

"Don't you have something to do…in the kitchen, maybe outside?" Olivia chided.

"My apologies." Michael bowed and backed his way out of the living room into the kitchen.

"He's a strange man," George said thoughtfully.

"Olivia and I prefer to call him mysteriously unique."

"He's a work in progress, like most men." Olivia laughed, scrunching up her nose.

"So," Ellie prompted, "the guests are going to be here soon. What can we do to help?"

George's gaze fell to the floor. "I've been thinking about all of this drama. I'm getting old, maybe it's just my time, Ellie. I've never blown up like that before. It was shameful." He shook his head. "Just shameful. I've been Santa here in Lana Cove for over forty years, before you were even born."

"And you still are, to me, to Olivia, to the people here in Lana Cove. Why would you say that it's your time? You know that's not true. You bring so much happiness and joy to people's lives—"

"Then why would they fire me from the mall? And now my reputation is ruined. You know how this world is; everything is perception. They don't even care about reality or the truth anymore."

"Did something happen at the mall? What reason did they give you for firing you? Why would they hire," she could barely bring herself to say the words, "another Santa?"

"Nothing! I'd been working at the mall just like always, when suddenly, out of the blue, I receive a phone call from Ed Reed's secretary telling me I was fired. A phone call, Ellie! They didn't even have the guts to tell me to my face."

"I'm so sorry," was all Ellie could muster, her mind searching for the right words to say, the right questions to ask.

"And, as if that wasn't the worst of it," George continued, "since that darn television station played that video, several of my biggest clients cancelled on me. I even lost the Bernstein account."

"Oh." Ellie felt like the wind had been knocked out of her.

The Bernstein Gala was an incredible annual event held at the Bernstein Mansion. A multi-million-dollar oceanfront estate that had been featured on the *Travel Channel* and *The Homes of the Rich and Famous* series. Every year the Bernsteins held a raffle, and fifty families were invited from around Lana Cove to come feast and celebrate Christmas. George had been a part of the celebration for the past twenty years.

"Robert...Mr. Bernstein," George clarified, "told me that the events on television would tarnish his reputation. He didn't want anything to ruin the pristine perception of his perfect party. So he hired the new Santa...Drew Small."

"Who the heck is this Drew Small guy? It's like he just appeared and all of a sudden he started claiming Santa rights."

"He doesn't even have a real beard!" George exclaimed. "But," he said, his face turning red, "you probably already know that."

"Yeah." Ellie smiled affectionately. "So, you have no idea who this guy is?"

"None, and believe me, I checked. He's not a member of the official Santa union, and he's not a member of the official Santa's Facebook page or the North Pole Answering service. The local post office brings children's letters—addressed to Santa—to me, and I answer them," George explained. He must have seen the confused expression on Ellie's face.

"That's really sweet. I had no idea that was even a thing."

"What's really sweet?" Olivia asked, balancing two trays of holiday cookies on her arms. "Don't say it, Michael," she yelled toward the kitchen.

"He was going to say *you are*, wasn't he?" George asked.

"If you look up predictable in the dictionary…."

"You'll find his picture." Ellie sighed.

"Guilty." Michael laughed, stepping into the living room, wiping his hands on his apron.

"George was telling me…." She paused and turned to George to make sure it was okay to continue.

He nodded and gestured for her to keep going.

"That a man named Drew Small took his job at the mall and the Bernstein Estate."

"Drew Small." Michael chuckled. "He's just lucky his first name isn't Richard." He glanced expectantly from Ellie to George to Olivia. "Not funny?"

"Not in the slightest," Ellie replied.

"Fine, how about the name Drew Small, sounds like someone who specializes in miniature works of art. A gunslinger with tiny pistols?"

"Currently he's specializing in making George's life miserable," Ellie chided, "and you're not helping."

"I'm belittling him, that's gotta be somewhat helpful. Fine, George, you said Ed Reed's secretary called and gave you the news. Did you try to get in touch with him personally?"

"Of course, Ed's an incredibly busy man. He's in charge of all of the special events around the city. He and I worked on the Santa extravaganza for years. I've tried calling, I've left messages, I've texted him. So far, nothing. I honestly don't know what happened."

"Were there any complaints? Any angry parents? Anything that would cause them to fire you?" Ellie inquired delicately.

"Nothing. I never heard so much as a peep of anyone being upset. I woke up Thursday morning, got dressed to go to the mall—and that's when I got the phone call, letting me know I'd been fired. I knew there had to be some kind of mistake. I tried to get Ed on the phone, but it kept going to his voicemail, so I headed to the mall to figure out what had happened."

"So, you were never able to talk to Ed in person?" Ellie prompted.

"No. That was the craziest part. Ellie, you don't just fire someone after forty years. I went to Ed's office, but Jan, his secretary, told me he wasn't there. I knew he was there. I could see a light under his door, and I saw his shadow under the doorway. Ed was there…."

"Okay, so Ed wouldn't talk to you, then what did you do?" Michael asked.

"Well, I figured if Ed wasn't going to talk to me, I would try to talk to the new Santa, you know, maybe he would be nice enough to at least tell me what was going on."

"Okay." Ellie nodded. "Go on."

"So…." George's face turned red. "I went to the men's restroom, across from the employee breakroom. I figured he'd have to come there and change. We weren't allowed to wear our Santa suit outside the mall," he clarified. "Imagine my surprise when this kid in his thirties comes in and dumps his Santa suit out onto the bathroom floor from a black trash bag. The disrespect…." George huffed. "He would have been kicked out of the NSU instantly. National Santa Union. That suit," George emphasized, "is sacred, and it's an honor to wear it."

"Completely understood." Ellie nodded again. "And you confronted Drew?"

"Well, not so much confronted him. I asked him how he got the job, and he told me to mind my own business."

"Did he know who you were?"

"No, not until I told him. I let him know that I was the original Santa and that I'd been fired. I told him I just wanted to know why. So instead of being a decent human being, the kid laughed in my face and told me to stop harassing him or he'd call security."

"Let me guess," Michael said, "you tried to reason with him."

"I asked him, nicely, if he had any idea why I was fired. He got all angry and said something like 'Suit yourself, old man.' He threw his trash bag to the floor and stormed out of the restroom. Next thing I know, two security guards showed up and asked me to leave, like I was a criminal or something."

"Only you didn't," Michael prodded gently.

"No, I know I should have…but as you know, hindsight is twenty-twenty. So, I went to my car and sat there. I should have left." George shook his head. "Because the longer I sat there, the angrier I got. Finally, I couldn't take it anymore, I just needed some answers, so I snuck in through the employee entrance, made my way to the winter wonderland set—the set that *I* created—and when I saw him, and the children and the elf…I just lost it. I wasn't trying to hurt the guy."

George stared at the floor. "The rest, well, you've seen the video. After that, I was escorted out of the building and banned from the mall."

"That's a bit much," Olivia said, angrily shaking her head.

"You devote so much of your life...and in the blink of an eye, it's taken away from you," Ellie exclaimed.

"Seems like ripping a beard off a person, parading around and waving it in the air like it's your enemy's head is frowned upon." George said.

"All right, guys, I don't get it. None of this makes sense. Ellie, you, Olivia, and George have lived here in Lana Cove for eons, more of a statement than a question," Michael explained. "George, you grew up here, and you're like a hundred years old."

Ellie flashed an annoyed look at Michael.

"Okay, fine, ninety," Michael apologized. "My question is, do *any* of you know if there is a family of Smalls living in Lana Cove?"

The group immediately shook their heads in unison.

"So," Michael continued, "this guy just shows up, to a small town and starts taking all of the Santa gigs and besmirching our friend? No one sees this as being incredibly odd?"

"Yes, but a huge part of our community is made up of transplants. You showed up and said you quit your job in Boston, and gave up everything to become a mystery writer, and no one thought that was strange," Olivia pointed out.

"Well, of course not, just look at me, I am the literal personification of a successful writer, so not too much of a stretch there. Plus, my job doesn't require me to dress up as a fictional character, and it doesn't only pay one month out of a year."

"True." Olivia bobbed her head. "Yours pays in imaginary money—from the future."

"I came here to start a new life after a horrible divorce, and to begin a noble career as a bestselling author. Not that being Santa isn't noble," Michael confirmed, nodding to George. "All I'm trying to say is, Drew is new. I didn't do that rhyme on purpose, I'm just a natural wordsmith. We need to find out who he's connected with here, and why he's actually here. It would be a mistake to just think it's a coincidence."

"I hate to say it," Ellie nearly choked on her words, "but Michael's right."

Michael dropped his cookie to the floor. "Could you give me just a second? I need to find my phone…. Okay, got it. Could you please repeat the part where you said Michael is right? Feel free to add any embellishments you deem necessary."

Ellie continued her questions, ignoring Michael. "Does Drew have family here? How did he get the job at the mall? How did he get a job at the Bernstein's residence? How did they even hear about him?"

"Exactly," Michael concurred, "you completed my thoughts perfectly. If he's not staying with family, where is he staying? And why Santa? Does he have another job? You said there was an elf with him, who is she? If I were doing character research for a book, I would want to know all of those things."

Olivia glanced out the front window. A set of headlights turned off the road and pulled into Michael's driveway.

"The guests are beginning to arrive," she announced.

"That's my cue," George said. "Where would you like me to change?"

"In the guest bedroom," Michael responded. "It's the second door on the right. There's a bathroom in there, and a treadmill should you get the urge to work off a few pounds."

"George." Ellie placed her hand gently on his arm as he walked away. "We'll get to the bottom of this. But tonight, I want you to know that you are surrounded by friends and people who love you. Let's have a good night tonight, and we'll begin sorting things out first thing in the morning."

"Thank you, Ellie…and you too, Olivia." George smiled affectionately.

"What about me?" Michael asked, clearly feeling left out.

"Two lumps of coal for you." George laughed as he disappeared down the hallway to get ready. "Two lumps of coal."

"I like him." Michael grinned. "A consummate professional, already in character."

"Two lumps of coal," George's voice rang out again from the guest room.

Chapter 3

It was the perfect night for a Christmas party. A steady snow was falling, covering Lana Cove under a pristine, cottony blanket of white. Olivia had transformed Michael's living room into a Christmas work of art. Candles were flickering in the windows, a rainbow of lights twinkling on the Christmas tree. The faux fireplace was adorned with stockings, and old-fashioned lanterns glowed on either side of the hearth.

Olivia had just finished lighting candles on the beautifully decorated table when the doorbell rang.

"I'll get it," Ellie chirped as she opened the door for the newly arrived guests. "Andrew, Denise." She gave them each a kiss on the cheek. "Come in, come in. I *love* that houndstooth jacket," she gushed. "It's gorgeous."

"Thank you, Ellie. Hi, Michael," Denise said, waving.

Ellie moved aside and turned her head toward Michael. "Oh God," she gasped.

"What?" Michael asked innocently, proudly sporting a bright-red Christmas sweater adorned with flashing colorful lights, green pants, and white patent-leather shoes. He wasn't sure, but he swore envy filled Andrew's eyes.

"Michael," Ellie stammered, "what are you wearing? It's...it's...."

"Breathtaking?" Michael prompted. "Exquisite?"

"Abysmal." She groaned.

"What are you talking about, El? He looks dashing," Andrew replied, winking at Michael.

"See?" Michael gloated, empowered by Andrew's comments. He plucked a curly pipe from his pocket and tapped it on his pants leg. "What now?" He shrugged and gave Ellie a confused glance. "It's not a real pipe. It just adds an air of sophistication."

"Is that George's pipe?" Olivia asked.

"No." Michael stared at her indignantly. "Okay, well, yes, I may have accidentally removed it from his Santa jacket when I gave him a hug."

"You're incorrigible," Ellie cried. "Why can't you dress like Andrew? Look at him: Burberry scarf, beautiful gray coat, black slacks. It's like he just stepped out of a *GQ* photo shoot."

Andrew tugged up his pants leg, revealing a bright-red pair of socks with reindeer. A mischievous, childlike grin filled his face.

"Well," Olivia checked out Andrew's socks, "they are both festive and tasteful."

"Don't forget to add whimsical," Andrew piped in.

"Your outfit," she said, facing Michael, "well, there aren't any words."

"Hah? Your jealousy is palatable. Pure beauty is indescribable," Michael retorted. He would have continued had the doorbell not interrupted him. "Saved by the bell," he muttered defensively.

The living room bubbled with conversation and laughter. There was something about Christmas music that made people happy. A rollicking game of Secret Santa found Michael relinquishing his sweater in exchange for Andrew's reindeer socks. Michael considered himself the victor—he had all but lusted over Andrew's socks.

As the adults settled down, clustered in tiny groups, Olivia grabbed a glass and pinged it with a fork. She smiled, seemingly a little embarrassed by all of the sudden attention. "Well!" She laughed. "That was a lot more effective than I thought it would be." She glanced around the room, addressing the children. "We have a special guest tonight."

The children stared at her with rapt attention.

"Who?" Cindy asked, a little brown-haired, brown-eyed girl, incredibly adorable in her plush green-and-silver dress.

Olivia nodded at Michael. The children let out a chorus of dejected moans when they saw him.

"No, no, no, not him, someone *special*," Olivia said.

Michael played the first notes of *Santa Claus is Comin' to Town* on his piano.

The children's eyes flew wide open, and Cindy held her hand over her mouth, barely covering her *Oh!* expression.

"Is it Santa Claus?" she whispered shyly.

Olivia couldn't take it; the little girl was just too cute. "I think so!" she nodded.

Cindy threw her hands together and jumped up and down as Michael played the song.

George's voice rang through the house. "Ho-ho-ho!"

And when he appeared in the living room, the children whispered, "Santa!"

Ellie glanced at Olivia. All of her childhood memories came flooding back to her. Just about every person in the room had visited George for Christmas. If there ever was a Santa...it was George.

The children danced around him and hugged him, their faces filled with pure delight. Joy lit George's eyes. He took a seat in front of the fireplace and removed a beautifully illustrated *The Night Before*

Christmas book from his satchel. Everyone gathered around, listening to him read the story. Not a creature was stirring, not even a mouse.

When he was finished, George closed the book and smiled at the children. He leaned forward. The children scooched closer; they couldn't take their eyes off him. "I've got a gift for each of you. Now remember," he said softly, "Christmas isn't for a couple more days, but since all of you have been so good this year…well, except for Michael," he winked. He held his hand up to his mouth and whispered, "He's on my naughty list."

The children gasped, and adults broke into laughter.

"Maybe if he tries really hard over the next couple days," Santa joked playfully, "I'll have the elves make him something."

The children nodded in agreement. A small boy crossed his arms and added, "*If* he behaves."

George reached into his satchel and gave each child a candy cane and a gift, wrapped in silver paper with a blue ribbon.

"And for the parents, so you can start a tradition with your children…." He handed each of the adults an illustrated copy of *The Night Before Christmas*.

Cindy looked at her gift and then at Michael. She turned and said something quietly in Santa's ear. He nodded and dug in his bag, handing her another copy of the book. Cindy proudly marched over to Michael and gave it to him. The girl pulled on Michael's shoulder, and he leaned in toward her.

"I told Santa that everyone needs something special on Christmas," she said quietly.

Her voice tickled Michael's ear, and for a moment he disappeared back to that place, when his daughter held his hand and whispered in his ear.

"Thank you." Michael hugged Cindy. "Thank you so much."

"Try to be good, okay?" Cindy said as she walked away.

George caught Ellie's eye. He mouthed *thank you* and then bid farewell to everyone as *I'll Be Home for Christmas* began to play.

Chapter 4

Olivia stretched and rubbed her hands across her legs. Her bright-red nose matched her scarlet fuzzy earmuffs. "It's freezing out there."

"It's thirty-one." Michael nodded, took a bite of his egg-and-cheese croissant, and flipped open his laptop. "Supposed to snow until this evening." He wiped his mouth off on his sleeve.

"You're such a Neanderthal," Olivia chided, sliding a napkin over to him.

"Hey, don't disparage Neanderthals." Ellie laughed. She wrapped her fingers around her coffee mug for warmth. "So, what's the plan? Livs and I have to work until three."

"You own this place…can't you give yourself a break? What about the millennial?" Michael tilted his head toward the pale, thin male in a white button-down shirt and black skinny jeans. "Can't he stay a little late?"

"He pulled a double yesterday. He said he has to have time to go to Soul Cycle and Christmas shopping for his family."

"Soul Cycle? He's so thin he could wear my watch as a belt."

"Leave Dwayne alone, he's a sweetie, and a hard worker. Trust me, those are difficult to come by nowadays."

"Okay, while you and Olivia are prodding your customers for clues, I'm going to do some recon work at the mall. Hopefully I'll be able to find out a bit more about Drew."

"All right, give us a buzz if you discover anything. We'll do the same. Also," Ellie said, grabbing Michael's arm as he stood, "don't do anything stupid. I spent all of my bail money on presents."

"I'll do my best," Michael promised and headed toward the counter.

Michael eased off of the A1A highway onto Mall Drive. For a smallish-sized town, the Lana Cove Mall was a cornucopia of big-name stores as well as boutique shops that catered to the more sophisticated connoisseur—the type of person who wouldn't think twice about dropping a couple hundred dollars on candles with names like 'vanilla pumpkin' or 'cinnamon latte.'

Michael eased his red Miata into the mall parking lot. It was a lightweight car and didn't handle well in the snow. He drove along the outer loop and parked at the back of the Macy's department store. The yearly Santa Extravaganza was hosted by Macy's, so it made sense to Michael that Drew would park at the back entrance.

He took a sip of coffee and flicked his wipers twice, clearing the snow off his windshield. Bright-orange plows, their amber lights flashing, were busy creating mountains of snow. An older woman clambered out of her car, one arm wrapped tightly around her coat, the other clutching her hat. The wind had picked up, gusting across the parking lot. Her scarf danced behind her like the tail of a kite.

Christmas wreaths with red ornaments swung back and forth, clanging on the light posts.

A steady stream of employees arrived, leaning against the wind, slipping and sliding as they made their way into Macy's back entrance. Michael grabbed a blueberry bagel from his bag and flicked the windshield wipers again. A metallic-blue Honda Accord pulled into a parking space, a few cars to his left. He stopped chewing and leaned forward.

There was quite a bit of commotion in the front seat of the Honda, and then a man in jeans and a black jacket hopped out of the driver's side. He opened the back door and tugged out a black trash bag.

"That must be Drew," Michael whispered to himself. *I see he hasn't upgraded his luggage,* he referred to the black bag where George had told them Drew kept his Santa suit.

A woman in a puffy white coat and brown leggings joined him. She looked like a marshmallow on a stick.

Michael grabbed his phone and fired off a quick text to Ellie. A few moments later, the words *I can't afford bail* appeared on his phone, with an emoji of a bag of money.

He rolled his eyes and watched Drew and the marshmallow lady disappear inside the mall. *I'll give them five minutes. Just enough time to finish my coffee and bagel.*

Michael was a professional. He could blend into any environment. He checked his surroundings and then gently pushed his car door open. A gust of wind buffeted the car, slamming the door on his leg.

"Mother Mary," Michael gasped, yanking his leg back inside. He raised his knee against his chest and sat for a long while, rocking. Finally, after the pain had abated, he cinched up his pants leg, quite certain the only thing that had kept him from severing his foot were the festival holiday socks he had won from Andrew at the Christmas party.

Assured that he would indeed walk again, he studied himself in the rearview mirror and adjusted his black baseball cap, drawing it low on his forehead. He narrowed his eyes. He had to admit, he was ruggedly handsome. Michael shoved the car door open, stepping lithely to the side. Just as he praised his athleticism, another gust of wind tore his baseball cap from his head, sending it skittering across the parking lot.

Michael sighed, watching his favorite cap disappear beneath a row of cars. He quickly walked across the parking lot, to Drew's car, wincing with every step.

The first thing Michael spotted was the barcode on the back window. *Rental car.* He moved to the rear and fished out his phone. *Florida plates.* He swiped to his photo app and snapped a picture.

I wonder if…. He tried the handle of the passenger door. *Locked.* He tried the driver and passenger doors, all locked. Of course it wouldn't be that easy. He held his phone to his face, as if making a phone call, and scanned the parking lot. With the wind and the snow, it was nearly impossible to see anything.

Satisfied he wasn't being observed, Michael reached inside his pocket and removed a small inflatable black bag, about the size of a plastic sandwich bag. It was connected to a thin tube, with an egg-shaped inflator attached to it. It worked like a miniature bicycle pump. He carefully inserted the edge of the bag between the door and the doorframe, and inflated it. Satisfied, he removed a thin rod—that looked like a collapsible pointer with a rubber tip—from his pocket.

He poked it inside the space created by the inflatable bag and maneuvered the stick south until it hovered just above the door's unlock button. He pressed downward, and a satisfying metallic click sounded as the door released.

Like a pro. Michael smiled. He quickly removed the inflator and collapsible rod, and slipped into the passenger's side of Drew's car. Settling into the cold vinyl seat, he opened the glove box. It was nearly empty except for the owner's manual and, the coup de grâce, the Hertz rental agreement.

Hello, Mr. Calvetti. He pulled out his phone and took pictures of the rental agreement. Michael opened the center console; it was filled with gum and candy bar wrappers.

"What's this?" Michael flipped over a circular card with a hook at the top, meant to be hung from the rearview mirror. "Parking pass for the Beach Comber Motel dated from November twelfth through December twenty-seventh." He quickly peered beneath the seats and in the trunk, but there was nothing else of interest.

Michael hurried back to his car, pushed the start button, and flicked on the seat warmers. He swiped his finger across the screen of his phone and clicked on Ellie.

She answered after the third ring. "Well, your call isn't coming from a payphone, so I'm guessing you're not in jail."

"Sorry to disappoint. I can hear the concern in your voice, and I gotta tell you, it's heartwarming."

"So. Whaddya got? We're slammed."

"A few things," Michael replied. The commotion of the café filtered through his phone. "First, Drew's real name is Drew Calvetti."

"Calvetti. Interesting, unless it's an alias. He could be using a stolen identity."

"Maybe. I'll know for sure as soon as I get back to my office and run a background check on him. He listed a Virginia address and phone number. I also found a parking pass for the Beach Comber Motel."

"The Beach Comber…. That's a good choice if you are trying to fly under the radar. You can pay cash there, and it's kind of a 'don't ask, don't tell' establishment."

"Hmm, interesting you know so much about it. Almost like—"

"I've never stayed there. I've lived here my whole life. Wait, why am I explaining myself to you?"

"I don't know, guilty conscience? I do have one of those faces where people love to tell me their deepest, darkest secrets. Anything else you'd care to divulge?" He waited a few beats and then continued. "How about you guys, learn anything new?"

"Nothing we didn't already know after talking to George. I'll let you know if we find out anything substantial."

"Okay, sounds good. I'm going to head home and see what I can dig up on Mr. Calvetti."

"Good luck!"

"You, too." He ended the call, flicked on his lights and windshield wipers, and pulled out of the parking lot onto Mall Drive, anxious to discover who the man was behind the fake beard.

Chapter 5

Ellie, Olivia, and Michael followed the hostess to a tall table at the back of Rumor's Bar and Grill. A jazz band played holiday favorites with a thumping baseline and masterful piano playing.

"Wow," Olivia exclaimed, gesturing toward the band dressed in red blazers, gold shimmering ties, and green pants, "they're really good."

"Yeah," Ellie said. "I love those upright basses, such a unique sound."

"I used to play the bass," Michael said, his face serious.

"Really?" Ellie asked.

Michael could tell from her expression she was impressed. "Yes, until I broke my G-string."

Olivia shook her head. "Ellie, you should know by now."

Ellie was about to respond when a young Asian woman in a white button-down shirt and black skirt arrived at their table. "Hello, everyone, I'm Jen, I'll be your server tonight. May I interest you in a cocktail, an appetizer?"

"It's a cold, wintery night," Ellie mused. "I think I'll have a Moscow Mule."

"Nice," Olivia replied, "make that two."

"And you, sir?"

"I'll take an Old Fashioned, with Maker's Mark. Oh, and plenty of cherries."

"Would you like a sweater vest with that and some reading glasses?" Ellie teased.

"Funny." Michael shook his head and sighed. "The truth is, Jen, they fight over me constantly. Honestly, it's embarrassing. I told them, it's Christmas, just put a big red bow on me, and, well…." Michael smiled. "No need to bore you with the details."

"I think I just lost my appetite." Ellie groaned.

"So…," Michael clasped his hands together as the waitress walked off. "Any juicy news?"

"A smidgen. Mrs. Mallory…."

Michael shrugged, clueless as to who they were talking about.

"She was a professional golfer, a wing of the country club is named after her," Ellie added, giving the story some much-needed context.

"Oh, *that* Mrs. Mallory." Michael nodded and gestured for Ellie to continue.

"Someone stole a thirty-thousand-dollar diamond necklace from her house."

"Whoa." Michael whistled. "A break-in? Inside job? When did it happen?"

"That's just it," Olivia answered. "She's uncertain. There was no sign of a break-in, and she's not sure when it went missing."

"What?" Michael shook his head. "She's not sure how long it's been missing? It's a thirty-thousand-dollar necklace," he continued. "How would you *not* know it's missing?"

"It's not like she wore it every day, Michael. When she opened her safe, it was missing, along with her passport, and some other less valuable pieces of jewelry," Ellie explained.

"She must have a sophisticated alarm system. I've seen her house; that thing is like a fortress."

"The police didn't find any signs of forced entry, and the alarm company didn't find anything unusual either," Olivia added.

"Then it had to be an inside job—but…," Michael continued his thought, "once inside, how did the thief get into her safe? I'm only asking because I assume she probably has a pretty substantial one."

Ellie made a face. "She's not sure that it was even locked. You know how people get. She's lived in that house for sixty years—she just never thought it would be a problem."

"It's never a problem until it's a problem," Michael declared sagely.

"You get that off a cereal box?" Olivia teased.

"No, from Mr. Lambert, my psychology professor. He said people find safety through repetition and routines. Unfortunately, routines establish a predictable pattern which can be exploited."

"Jeesh, Michael." Ellie winked. "You actually sounded smart for a minute. Don't make that a habit."

"I just reread his lecture notes a couple weeks ago while doing research on a jewelry thief for my book. Most of the people who he robbed had a false sense of security. He would find thousands of dollars' worth of jewelry simply lying out in the open."

"I can relate. I can't tell you how many times I've gone to sleep at home with my windows open and my doors unlocked. I just feel safe here." Olivia shrugged.

"Did the police have suspects? Anything to go on?" Michael asked.

"Well, without a timeline, it's difficult—and it doesn't help that she has a busy social schedule. She hosts a weekly book club, afternoon tea, and an annual Thanksgiving and Christmas party."

"That's a lot of opportunity," Michael said.

"And with so many people having access to her house…." Ellie spread her hands as if laying out her cards.

"Well…if I had to bet my vast, nonexistent fortune on who did it, I would have to bet it was someone during her Thanksgiving extravaganza," Michael suggested.

"She probably has the same group that shows up every week for her book club, and the same friends who show up for tea. It would be too much of a risk for any of them to take it," Ellie added.

Olivia agreed. "But it would also have to be someone who knew her, who knew about the necklace."

"Or someone who just got lucky—someone who had access to her house and just decided to do a little snooping. Was the Thanksgiving party catered?" Michael asked. "Because that would be a good way to…. Over your shoulder." Michael motioned at Ellie as Jen leaned in between her and Olivia and put two copper mugs on the table.

She gave Michael an ironic smile and popped a beautifully glassed drink in front of him, a mountain of maraschino cherries spilling over the top onto the table.

"Finally," Michael gasped, "a woman who understands me."

While he fawned over his new treasure trove of cherries, Ellie ordered the sea bass with capers and lemon garlic butter. Olivia opted for grilled chicken breast, with broccoli and Yukon potatoes, and finally returning to the grown-up world, Michael chose a Caesar salad with grilled chicken.

Olivia took a sip of her Moscow Mule and turned to Michael. "So, we filled you in. What did you learn about Mr. Calvetti?"

"And don't tell us again that his name rhymes with spaghetti, it's not funny," Ellie added.

Olivia nodded in agreement.

"Oh yeah." Michael placed his hand over his mouth, finishing chewing his salad. "Thank you, Olivia, I got so wrapped up in Mrs. Mallory's fascinating story I forgot about my news." He gestured for everyone to lean in. "It seems Mr. Calvetti has quite the record. He's done time for assault, burglary, grand theft auto, bank fraud, and…from the court records I found, he has ties to the Calvetti crime family."

"That's some big-time crime."

"Nicely put, Livs." Michael smiled.

"So," Ellie said, mulling through this new information, "if he has such an extensive record, how did he get a job as Santa at the mall? I know they do background checks. And I hardly doubt that he's built up a fake backstory as Drew Small."

"I agree." Olivia nodded. "Think about it. How could he get a gig at the Bernstein's party? Mr. Bernstein runs checks on all of his employees."

"All good questions," Michael said. "At the moment, all I can think of is that he assumed someone else's identity. Maybe there is an actual law-abiding citizen named Drew Small, and that's who he's passing himself off as."

"What are the chances of there being two Drews?" Olivia asked.

"I don't know," Michael said, "I'm just spit-balling. But one thing I do know is, I'm going to have a talk with Ed Reed tomorrow. Once he finds out who Drew really is…I don't think he's going to be the go-to Santa much longer."

"And George could get his job back!" Olivia's face filled with hope.

"I'm not so sure," Michael said. "That news story was pretty damaging."

Olivia's face fell.

"But you never know," Michael added quickly, "he and Ed have known each other for a long time. Maybe he'll have a change of heart."

"I hope so. Right now, none of this is making sense."

"I can see the connection," Ellie said. "If Drew is running or hiding from the law, he would assume a new identity. The jewelry would provide him with the cash that he needs. My guess is once he gets what he wants, he's going to bolt out of town."

"So you think he stole Mrs. Mallory's necklace?" Michael asked.

"I'm not sure yet...," Ellie took a sip of her drink. "But things didn't start happening until he showed up."

"Maybe he's just here trying to start his life over again," Olivia suggested. "I mean, move to a small town, try to blend in and all. If I was trying to hide, and then George started asking me questions, I would probably respond the same way. A job playing Santa would enable him to get some money and perhaps work his way back into society."

"It just doesn't feel right," Ellie said. "I want to know why George got fired from his job. How Drew got his job, and how he landed his gig at the Bernstein's. It's too convenient for all of these things to fall into place for Drew."

"Hi, Jen," Michael said, looking up, suddenly aware she was standing at the table. "Everything is wonderful, thank you."

"Oh good, good." She nodded. "I'm sorry, sir, but is your name Michael West?"

"Why yes, it is." He puffed up his chest. "I'm such a great writer," he explained to Olivia and Ellie, "that she already knows me before my first book is even published." He took the piece of paper from her hand and scribbled his name on it. "There you go. Save that—it's going to be worth a fortune someday."

"Thank you." Jen smiled awkwardly. "Actually…," she handed the paper back to him, "a man just asked me to give this to you."

Olivia snorted into her drink.

"Oh, yes, of course, thank you, Jen. Fans come in all shapes and sizes."

"What is it, Michael?" Ellie said. "Did he ask for your number? Fashion advice?"

"No," Michael said, suddenly serious. "Someone has information. Jen," he called out, stopping her. "I'm so sorry…." He waved her back to the table. "But who gave this note to you?"

"A man in a black overcoat. He was wearing a hat and glasses. He gave me fifty dollars and asked me to deliver the note to you."

"Has he ever been in here before? Is he a local?" Ellie inquired.

"I told him I wouldn't say who he was." Jen's voice faltered. "He said it was very important, and I promised him. He didn't threaten you, did he?" Her eyes suddenly flew wide open.

"No, no. Everything is fine, it was just peculiar. Everything is fine." Michael smiled, reassuring her again.

"Are you sure?" she asked hesitantly.

"Yes." Michael smiled harder. "You kept your word, that's a trait rarely found these days."

Jen thanked the group and walked away. Michael could tell she was battling with herself, trying to figure out if she'd done the right thing.

"You gonna clue us in," Ellie asked, "or keep us in suspense?"

He slid the paper over to Ellie and Olivia.

It read: *I have information. Call me.*

Followed by a phone number.

Chapter 6

Michael and Olivia piled into Ellie's Silver Acura ILX.

"Oh my God," Olivia stammered, "it's freaking freezing in here."

"Give me a second." Ellie started the car and cranked the heat up to high. "It warms up fast."

"Sounds like the last words someone says before they freeze to death," Olivia exclaimed through chattering teeth.

"All right," Michael said, "I'm going to call our mysterious stranger." He jabbed the digits into his phone and selected speaker.

Moments later, a raspy voice answered.

"Hello?" Michael asked, not sure what to expect.

"Is this Michael West?"

"Yes...."

"Where are you now?"

"If the next question is *what are you wearing?*— I'm gonna insist on you buying me a drink," Michael replied.

"Last chance, Mr. West," the caller demanded.

"Fine, I'm about to leave Rumor's restaurant, but you already knew that…."

"Meet me in ten minutes at the Ocean Deck. Last booth on the left, beneath the swordfish. Come alone."

"Why can't you…?" Michael was speaking to a dead line.

"You aren't going to really go there and meet him, are you? It could be Drew. It could be a trap!" Olivia said.

"It's not Drew…and I don't think it's a trap."

"How do you know? He could have easily disguised his voice."

"I know, because Jen knew him, and I trust Jen's gut."

"You're trusting someone you don't even know?"

"Even if it isn't Drew," Ellie surmised, "it could be a crazy person, maybe even someone dangerous from Drew's past."

"First of all, the Ocean Deck is usually crowded, so there will be plenty of people around. Secondly, if this was a dangerous person from his past searching for him, all he would need to do is show up at the mall. He's pretty easy to spot."

"Is there a thirdly?" Olivia asked. "Because bad news always seems to come in threes."

"Yes, it's obvious Jen knows who he is…and I'm betting we probably know who he is as well. He just wants to meet in a place a little less conspicuous. There is bad news, though," Michael continued. "I have to make it all the way to beachside in seven minutes now, in rush-hour traffic."

"But we don't…,"Olivia turned toward the highway as a single car passed by "…have traffic."

"I'll switch on FaceTime," Michael said as he climbed out the backseat. "That way you can listen in."

"Good idea." Ellie nodded. "And, Michael, don't do anything stupid."

"It's the Ocean Deck." Michael shrugged. "What could possibly go wrong?"

Ellie and Olivia followed Michael's red Miata down A1A past rows of condos and hotels, all fighting over prized real estate, facing the ocean.

Ellie was born in Lana Cove. She hated the thought of beautiful beachfront land being bought up by developers. As oceanfront parcels became available, the citizens of Lana Cove fought back against greedy investors by purchasing land, so they couldn't build.

"Ellie…Ellie," Olivia was talking.

Michael's right turn signal flashed red, like a winking cyclops with hay fever.

"Sorry." Ellie smiled, deep in thought for a moment.

"Let's park at the iHop. That way we're right across the street from the Ocean Deck if Michael needs us."

"Sounds good." Ellie braked and waited for a car to pass, then pulled into the lot. She'd just parked when her phone rang. She pressed 'accept.' Michael's smiling face appeared on her screen. "Hey, handsome."

"Hey, Ellie, I'm going to put my phone in my front pocket. Hopefully you'll be able to hear me okay."

"All right," Ellie said. "Good luck and be smart."

"Guys, I'll be fine. You're dealing with a trained professional. See you in a bit."

"Michael! Michael!"

Ellie's phone rang again.

"Sorry, I hung up," he said.

"No kidding." Ellie looked over at Olivia, who was making the sign of the cross over her chest.

🌲🌲🌲🌲

Michael stepped into the doorway of the Ocean Deck and paused, allowing for his senses to catch up to the garish interior. The smell of fried and battered food filled the air, congealing with Bob Seger belting out that he *still loves that old-time rock and roll.*

Michael tilted his head, checking out the long row of picnic tables covered in red-and-white checkered tablecloths. Greasy menus lay against the wall, festooned between ketchup and mustard squeeze bottles. In the center of the table stood a beautifully ornate metallic stand, supporting a Jenga-sized tower of wet wipes. A card on the table let customers know they could request bibs if they ordered crabs or lobster.

A smattering of patrons sat at the bar watching Sports Center. Michael navigated to the rear of the restaurant, where a man in a black jacket and black stocking cap sat with his back to him, beneath a giant swordfish named Eddie.

The mysterious man motioned for Michael to sit across from him—he kept his head down, staring at his beer. One of Michael's exercises as a writer was to break down the components of a character: their demeanor, their clothing, and their idiosyncrasies. The old saying, actions speak louder than words, usually turned out to be true.

Whoever this man was, he didn't want to meet Michael's eyes. He hid his identity behind a stocking cap pulled low over his eyebrows. Thick black glasses perched on his nose, and he had a mustache that Michael was pretty sure was fake. His hands were tan, even in the middle of winter, which told Michael that he must spend a lot of time outside, perhaps fishing or boating.

"Put your phone on the table." The man gestured to the tabletop. He had a raspy voice, that itchy sound you usually only heard from lifelong smokers or people who drank too much dairy.

"What?" Michael wasn't sure he'd heard the man right.

"You heard me, put your phone on the table. I want to make sure no one else is listening in."

Michael gave the man an appalled expression and then slowly fished his phone out of his pocket, making sure to press the 'end call' button. Just to annoy the man, he placed it face down on the table. The man grabbed it and flipped it over.

A woman in jeans and a black t-shirt appeared at the table, her arms and neck covered in tattoos. The man dipped his head, and she placed a beer in front of Michael and walked off.

"Thank you," Michael said. "So, I obviously received your message. You said that you had information for me?"

"I do. I'm only talking to you because I think you have George's best interest at heart."

"Of course I do," Michael said. "He's a good friend. I think what happened to him is horrific."

"I do, too, and I'm risking a lot just talking to you, so when I'm finished, I'm going to walk away. Sit and finish your beer, and then leave. Understood?"

"Understood," Michael said solemnly.

"Do you know Ed Reed?"

"I know of him. George mentioned him, but I don't know him personally."

"Mr. Reed has a lot of influence locally. His brother is the head of the town council. Most people don't know it, but he pulls the strings for many local businesses—and he has a lot of connections."

"Okay." Michael cleared his throat. "I get it. Powerful and influential, thumbs in a lot of people's pies."

"Exactly." The man pulled out his cell, swiped across the screen, and then slid it across the table to Michael.

Michael stared at the man's phone, and his heartbeat quickened. "May I?"

The man nodded.

Michael stared at the first image and then zoomed in. "That's Mr. Reed and the elf."

"Swipe once more," the man replied.

Michael swiped forward. He immediately recognized Drew's car. A figure was crouched in the backseat with a camera, taking pictures. Although the figure in the image was blanketed in shadow, Michael could tell it was Drew. "How did you get these? Where were these taken?"

"At Luna's. Keep swiping, there's a few more."

"No," Michael gasped, "not the Honey Dew Motel." It was a cheap, by-the-night motel, with a less-than-reputable reputation. Picture after picture documented Ed Reed's indiscretion. There he was getting out of the car with the woman, then at the door of the motel, and then stepping into the room.

"Here's what's interesting." The man gestured to the phone. "See this next picture? That was taken two minutes after they went into the room."

"Doesn't say much for Mr. Reed." Michael chortled, then immediately regretted it, seeing the expression on the other man's face. "Sorry…vivid imagination," he said, tapping the side of his head.

"The point is, she dashed out of that room after two minutes. My guess is he made himself comfortable. She probably snapped a picture or two and then ran out."

"Wow." Michael exhaled and shook his head. "A set-up, and Drew documented the whole thing…. Pretty obvious now how he got the Santa gig and the Bernstein job." Michael slid the phone back to the man. "There is one thing I'm confused about. How did she get into Luna's? It's a members-only bar—you have to be invited by a member."

"Don't be naïve, Michael. She's a young, beautiful woman. For someone like that, the management tends to look the other way for obvious reasons."

"Yeah, I can understand that," Michael acknowledged, "but still…, Mr. Reed is married, and well-known. I'm sure that he's *very* cautious."

"You're right, but the woman was just as cautious, and very subtle. You see, Michael, just like you, I am a student of human behavior, and I've developed a rather, shall we say, keen eye of picking up things that are out of place. I was sitting at the far end of the bar enjoying a cocktail and a fine Cuban cigar when she came in. I noticed her because she hovered in the doorway for a moment. At first, I thought she was looking for a friend, but then she made her way to the bar and sat next to Ed.

"She completely ignored him for the first twenty minutes or so, but then they started conversing. She was good at playing the part of being disinterested…even James, the bartender, didn't give the two a second glance. I, too, was about to lose interest when she pulled her phone out of her purse.

"I assumed she was texting someone—until she laid her phone on the bar so he could read the screen."

"She was asking him to follow her, I'm guessing," Michael said.

The man took a sip of his beer. "Yes, he read whatever she wrote, nodded slightly, told James he had a million things to do, paid his tab, and left. She ordered another drink, sipped it for fifteen minutes or so, thanked James, and then paid her tab with cash and walked out."

"I wonder what she wrote. I mean, think about it. Ed Reed left the bar and waited outside for fifteen minutes. That's fifteen minutes of contemplating whether you're making the right decision." Michael leaned back in his seat and shook his head. "So, she blackmails Reed, he gives Drew the job, and…," Michael thought aloud, "calls Mr. Bernstein, asks him to hire Drew, and our friend George gets fired."

"Now you're getting the picture."

"Literally. But I don't understand," Michael said, puzzled. "Why are you showing me this? It's not going to help George get his job back, and the local news eviscerated the poor guy."

"I've lived in Lana Cove my entire life, as has George. I want you to find out what Drew is up to—and this woman—and expose them."

"It's pretty clear what's going on." Michael thought for a moment and decided to proceed. "Drew's real last name is Calvetti. He's got a list of crimes a mile long, grand theft, assault, bank fraud, you name it. I plan on visiting Ed tomorrow, but honestly, after seeing those pictures, I'm not sure Ed's going to roll over on Drew—he's got too much to lose."

"I agree…there are some very delicate things at play here, and I have to tread very carefully. I know your history. I know you're smart and tenacious. Drew is up to no good, and I feel that bigger things are at play here. I want you to find out what he's up to—if we can get him behind bars, then maybe we can save George and Ed."

He slid a thick envelope over to Michael.

"What's this?" Michael tapped it with a finger.

"An early Christmas present. Let's just call it an advance for your first book."

Michael pushed the envelope back to the man. "I can't take this."

"Oh, but you will, and you must, you must. I need you to clear George's name. This isn't just about his livelihood, it's about his reputation. We don't know what else Drew has done; we don't need Lana Cove's community to begin toppling like dominoes."

Without another word, the man shoved the envelope back to Michael, threw a twenty on the table, stood, and walked away.

Michael sat stunned as the man exited the bar. He opened the envelope and fanned through a thick wad of hundred-dollar bills. What the heck had just happened?

His phone buzzed. He flipped it over. A text from the mysterious man's phone—he'd sent him the pictures of Ed Reed with the woman.

Michael glanced around. No one seemed to be paying any attention to him. He touched Ellie's name and sent her a quick text: *On my way, I'm okay.*

Chapter 7

"I'm telling you, it was like something out of *The Twilight Zone*," Michael said, carrying three piping-hot cups of tea into the living room. "Be right back." He hurried into the kitchen and came back moments later with sugar, honey, and spoons.

"Can I give you a hand?" Olivia asked, watching Michael disappear into the kitchen for the third time.

"No, it's my last trip," he shouted. He returned with a plate stacked with pastries. "Harry and David cookies," Michael explained. "They're from my old boss in Boston. He's still trying to lure me back, one delicious treat at a time."

"That's nice." Ellie grabbed a coconut macaroon. "But he'll just have to accept the fact that you're ours now, so hands off."

"Agreed." Olivia laughed. "But let him down slowly so he keeps sending cookies."

"So," Ellie asked, "you said that you had hush-hush information. What did you find out?"

"Ladies, you're not going to believe this one. Our mystery man had photos of Ed Reed with the elf," Michael said.

"What kind of photos?" Ellie asked, knowing there was more to the story.

"These." Michael opened the images on his phone. "Swipe through them, they kind of speak for themselves."

"Is that Drew with a camera in the—?"

"Yep, Drew was sitting in another car, taking pictures of everything. He's blackmailing Ed. That's how he got the Santa gig, and I'm pretty sure Ed made a call and that's how Drew got the Bernstein gig."

"Wow, as long as he knows Drew has these…he's not going to do anything. These pictures will destroy Ed," Ellie stated.

"So what do we do, go to the police?" Olivia asked. "Say that we have proof that an ex-con is extorting Ed Reed? This whole thing could explode in our faces. I mean, if we bust Drew, who's to stop his assistant from sending those pictures to the news?"

"Yep," Michael said, "the whole thing could unravel like an ugly Christmas sweater. I wish blackmail worked in reverse. I mean, if you look at Ed, he has Bernie Sanders hair, massive eyebrows—which I have my own theory: that he's growing them out as a makeshift comb-over—and gargantuan teeth.

"We could tell the woman that if she doesn't back down, we'll release the pictures of her going to a hotel with him. Thusly destroying her street cred and saving Ed and his family simultaneously."

"Thank you, Michael. Now, do you mind if Olivia and I get back to the world of reality and figure out our next move?"

"Sure, yes, certainly. Where were we?"

"So far, all we know is that Drew is guilty of blackmailing Ed. If we could prove that he was behind the theft of Mrs. Mallory's necklace, then he'd be arrested. Then, most likely Ed's indiscretions wouldn't have to be made public."

"At this point, he may want to take the option of telling his wife that he was fooled by a professional con artist," Olivia surmised.

"It would be the noble, right thing to do," Michael acknowledged, "but I don't know if he has it in him. We don't really know anything about this guy."

"So we do nothing?" Ellie asked, exasperated. "And meanwhile, George looks like the town idiot, and this crazy convict is calling all the shots?"

"It's not like we're *not* doing anything," Michael insisted, "we're finding out everything we can about Drew, and we're trying to see if we can pin this other crime on him. And," he added, "I don't know Ed personally, but I'm sure he'll come to some sort of arrangement with Drew. He's not going to be under his thumb forever."

The trio jumped as a loud *knock, knock, knock* came from the back door.

Ellie and Olivia looked at Michael. He shrugged and jumped to his feet—he was just as confused as they were about this late-night visitor.

He hurried through the kitchen, followed by Ellie and Olivia, and flicked on the back light. George stood on his porch, dressed in his Santa suit, peering around anxiously.

"George," Michael blurted, throwing open the door. "Come in." He stepped aside as George rushed into the house, his face pale as if he'd seen a ghost, his eyes wild.

"George, are you okay?" Ellie grabbed his hand.

George turned to Ellie and whispered, "He's dead, Ellie, he's dead."

"Who's dead? George!"

"Drew's dead, and the police think I killed him."

"Why on earth would they possibly think that?"

"Turn on the news." He gasped. "It's all over the news."

Michael sprinted into the living room. "Where's the remote?" he shouted.

"On the coffee table," Ellie said and joined Michael in the living room.

Michael grabbed the remote and flicked through the channels to the local news. Olivia helped George onto the sofa and stood next to Michael in front of the television.

A newswoman stood on the side of the street beneath a spotlight, wrapped in a brown winter coat, stocking cap, and scarf. Snow swirled all around her. She pointed to a house surrounded by police officers and emergency workers. Television vans and police cars lined the street in front of a large Victorian-styled home.

"George," Ellie turned to him, "that's your house!"

George nodded and closed his eyes; it was a nightmare that would never end.

A cluster of CSU officials busily secured the crime scene. Yellow police tape stretched around the entirety of the property. The news cameraman zoomed in, showing a miniature sleigh being pulled by eight tiny reindeer. The sleigh was crushed, and on top of the sleigh, Drew's body.

"Oh my God." Ellie's hand flew to her mouth.

The camera moved from George's yard, back to the newswoman. "We're standing in front of the home of George Owens, longtime Lana Cove native, where the body of Drew Small was found."

George's picture appeared on the screen—the news station decided to use a picture from when the security guards had escorted him out of the mall.

"According to Officer Sergeant Reynolds, Drew Small was shot and then thrown from the second-story balcony." The reporter turned and gestured toward it.

The cameraman followed her commentary with his camera.

"And he crashed onto the sleigh below."

The cameraman mimicked the fall by zooming in on the balcony and quickly lowering the camera to the sled below. The camera then panned back to the news reporter.

"So far, the police are keeping tight-lipped about the details, however, an anonymous caller said that he saw Mr. Small arguing with Mr. Owens at the Schooners restaurant shortly before his death. We are still waiting for Mr. Owens's arrival. Police are asking—for anyone with any information regarding this crime or Mr. Owens's whereabouts—to please call the Lana Cove Police Department."

"George," Ellie pleaded, "what's going on? We know you didn't do this."

"No, no, for God's sake, Ellie. I had just finished up at the Bernstein party. I stopped to get gas and coffee at Waverly's. As I'm getting my coffee, I hear the name of my street on the news. I look up and see my house, surrounded by police on the television, and there's Drew, sprawled on top of my sled. I didn't know where to go, so I came here. I know it wasn't smart, but I panicked. I'm so sorry."

"It's okay, it's okay," Ellie assured him, "we'll figure this out."

"George, let me see your hand, it's bleeding," Michael said.

"It's nothing," George said a little too quickly, "I just slipped on some ice out back. Really, it's nothing."

"Olivia, there's a first-aid kit in the closet beside the bathroom, do you mind?"

"Not at all," Olivia said. She hurried off down the hallway.

"George, start from the beginning," Ellie suggested, taking a seat beside him on the sofa. "Tell us everything that happened."

"Okay." He nodded. "I was just sitting down to eat dinner when my phone rang. The number showed up as unknown, so I didn't answer it, but then they called again. I was going to fuss at whoever it was and tell them I was about to eat when the guy tells me that it's Drew—and that he needed to talk to me in person. He said to bring my suit and to meet him at Schooners right away if I wanted my job back. I got so excited, I figured maybe he had talked to Ed. To be honest, I didn't really care if it meant getting my job back."

"Of course," Michael said, "so you went to Schooners to meet him."

"Exactly. When I got there, he was in a panic, jumpy, looking all around. He tells me that I can have all of my Santa jobs back on one condition. He pulled out this black book and said that he needed me to give it to someone at the Bernstein party."

"What did you say?" Ellie asked.

"That part was easy—I told him no way. I mean, I had no idea what was in that book, or where it came from. Something about the whole thing just didn't seem right. He obviously wasn't expecting me to say no, because he threw me against the wall and told me I had to take the book.

"The look he had in his eyes…I was scared to death, I thought he was going to kill me. I tried to leave, but he shoved me against the wall again. I tripped and fell, and he ran out the door.

"I got to my feet; everyone in Schooners was staring at me. Everything seemed to be happening in slow motion. I followed him outside. He was running to his car. The elf girl was sitting inside with the motor running, revving the engine. He must have stepped on some ice or something, because he slipped and landed hard, smacking his head. Two men burst through the door behind me, chasing after him.

"He scrambled to his feet, jumped into the car, and they sped away. The two men climbed into a black Ford Mustang and tore out of the parking lot, following him. I hurried to my car. If they were coming back, I didn't want to be around. The ice was red with blood where he fell, and that's when I found this—I think it's some kind of memory card. He must have dropped it when he toppled."

"Drew dropped it?" Michael asked.

George nodded. "I'm pretty sure. I found it right where he fell."

"One sec," Michael said excitedly, "I'll get my laptop."

Olivia and Ellie cleared the coffee table as Michael disappeared upstairs. Moments later, he returned and placed his laptop on the table.

"Okay, let's see what we got," Michael said, pushing the memory card into the side of the computer.

Ellie, Olivia, and George huddled in a semicircle around him.

A folder appeared on the screen, simply named DCIM.

"What's DCIM?" George asked. "Some kind of code?"

"Nothing nefarious." Michael clicked on the folder. "It stands for Digital Camera Images." The folder opened, revealing rows of pictures and video files.

"That's Ed, and…that's not his wife," George declared. "That's the elf woman."

"It's the reason you were fired. Drew was blackmailing Ed Reed." The folder contained additional photos of Ed in various stages of undress, on the motel bed.

"Oh my Lord!" George gasped. "This is going to destroy his wife…his daughter."

"Michael, these aren't just pictures of Edward," Ellie said. "These are photos from the November Art Expo. I helped cater the event."

"And there's Mrs. Mallory," Olivia said, pointing at the screen. "She just had a thirty-thousand-dollar necklace stolen," she explained to George. "We think Drew is somehow connected, we're just not sure how yet."

Michael clicked forward to the next image.

"There's a close-up." Ellie jabbed her finger at the screen. "Not that I've seen a lot of thirty-thousand-dollar necklaces, but that certainly looks like one."

"It's stunning," Olivia said.

"So, she still had the necklace when this photo was taken.... Wasn't the expo at the beginning of November?" Michael asked.

"It was November seventeenth, my mom's birthday," Olivia said.

"So, Drew was in town then…according to his motel parking pass."

"And you think Drew stole it?"

"We do," Ellie replied. "These photos are pretty damning. See how he zoomed in on the necklace in this photo?"

"I have to admit, he did his research. People love to dress up and show off their wealth at the art expo. It's a virtual who's who of the social elite of Lana Cove," George acknowledged.

"There's another example." Olivia gestured to a picture of a woman in a cocktail dress and a stunning diamond tennis bracelet. "That bracelet must be worth at least ten thousand dollars."

"At least," Ellie said, clearly stunned by the vast collection of images. "He's got dozens of pictures of jewelry."

"Not only jewelry." Michael nodded. "But people's houses."

"That's Mrs. Mallory's home," Ellie interrupted, "and that's Robert Neilson's house, there's the Bernstein estate, the Bono house...."

"Who in the world is that?" Olivia asked.

The last two rows of photos showed a man dressed in khakis and a gray button-down shirt. He didn't look the part of a mover or a shaker, Drew's usual target. The man in the picture was gawking at the elf woman. In the next image he was handing her a beer and then helping her with her coat.

"I'm not sure." Ellie turned to her friends.

They all shook their heads.

"Check out the background," Olivia said.

Ellie and Michael leaned in closer. Two women sat at the bar, facing toward the man, staring angrily. One of the women was holding a phone in her hand, obviously taking pictures.

"Our mystery man has a wedding ring, too...," Ellie added.

"If those women are doing what I think they're doing, that man's belongings are going to be in his front yard when he gets home," Michael said. "Hell hath no fury like a woman scorned."

"How does he even fit into the picture?" Olivia asked. "He certainly doesn't appear to be rich."

"Not sure," Michael replied. "Have you ever seen him before, George?"

"Sorry." George shook his head. "He doesn't look familiar."

"Can you zoom in on that chair, Michael? If that's his jacket," Ellie gestured to a gray jacket draped over a chair behind the man, "it has a logo on it; it may give us some idea as to who he is."

Michael clicked on the magnifying glass icon, and, using the mouse, moved the image so the jacket was in the center of the screen. A burgundy patch with gray letters that spelled P.E.W. was attached to the sleeve.

Michael opened Google and typed the words *Lana Cove P.E.W.* into the search box. Seconds later, the return results revealed *Precision Electrical Works*. He clicked on the link. An aged website that appeared as though it had been designed as an after-school project loaded.

"Wow," Olivia said, "that's a lot of gray and red...."

Michael quickly skimmed the contents of the page. "They're a local company." He read a bit more. "They specialize in home and small business electrical installation and repair...and bingo, it seems our mystery man is none other than Tony Meyer, owner and electrical operations specialist."

"Why would Drew and his friend get involved with an electrical contractor?" Olivia asked.

"No idea...the man's obviously married, so there's the blackmail element."

"Unless," Ellie said, continuing her thought, "what if Drew needed an electrician's assistance to break into people's houses, like Mrs. Mallory's?"

"That actually makes sense. They get pictures of this guy," Michael said, "and they threaten to show his wife. All he has to do is help disable a couple of alarms...."

"And they'll *promise* to destroy the pictures," Ellie said.

"Drew was casting a dangerous net," Michael said. "This town isn't very big. I mean, there's no way he could have sustained this type of behavior in such a small community. It's like playing Russian roulette. Eventually—"

"Eventually, you're going to wind up dead," Olivia said matter-of-factly.

"That's right," Ellie said, "he probably thought that if he had enough dirt on influential people, that no one could touch him."

"So, who do you think killed him?" Olivia asked.

"If I had to guess," Michael said, "it would be the person who had the most to lose."

"You think it was Ed, don't you?"

Michael gave George a look that said he wasn't going to deny it.

"Here's the deal, I know Ed's a scoundrel and a jerk," George bellowed, "but I've known him and his family for nearly twenty years. This isn't something he's capable of doing."

"I hope not," Ellie reassured him, "but having Drew out of the way would certainly make his life a lot easier. He—"

"He didn't do it," George cut her off, crossing his arms over his chest defiantly. "I mean, for all you know, it could have been me."

"George!" Ellie glared at him sternly. "Why would you say that?"

"Ed's a lot of things, but he's not a murderer."

"Well," Ellie sighed, "at least you have an airtight alibi. You were at the Bernstein's house when all of this happened, and you've got dozens of witnesses."

"Was Ed at the party, George?" Olivia asked.

"I don't know, I can't remember. There were so many people there...and I was still pretty rattled from the incident at the Schooners. I'm sure he was."

"I hate to say it," Michael said, "but right now George is most likely the prime suspect."

"Michael!" Ellie snapped, "What are you doing?"

"Ellie," Michael held up his hands, "please let me explain. Right now, the police have no idea about Ed being blackmailed, they have no idea about Tony being blackmailed—the last person who witnesses saw with Drew alive was George. This memory card shows that multiple people had motive to kill Drew.

George, we're going to have to turn this over to the police."

"I know…," George replied quietly.

"Do you have a good lawyer?" Michael asked. "The police are going to want to question you."

George's face turned pale.

Ellie reached out and took his hand. It felt cold and frail. "You're going to be fine." She smiled gently. "You have a strong alibi, and the memory card is going to show the police what Drew was up to."

George nodded. "You're right, Ellie, I just don't want anything to happen to Ed or his family. I'll give Gordon Sparks a call; he'll know what to do."

"You can use my guest room if you would like some privacy," Michael offered.

"Thank you." George squeezed Ellie's hand, retraced his steps down the hallway to the guest room, and shut the door.

"Look," Michael said when they were alone. "I know that George thinks Ed is innocent, but honestly, I think he's the prime suspect. We know it's not George, and it couldn't be Mrs. Mallory—

she could barely lift a five-pound bag of sugar—and her husband, well, he wears Izod Lacoste sweaters, so enough said."

"It could be Tony, the electrical worker," Olivia suggested.

"Maybe," Ellie said, "but from what we saw, he was acting like a total imbecile, but it didn't escalate to the same level as Ed...well," she corrected herself, "at least we don't have evidence that he went as far as Ed."

"We're forgetting a huge piece of the puzzle," Olivia exclaimed, "the black book."

"That's right." Ellie nodded. "He tried to get George to deliver the book to someone at the party."

"Which meant Drew couldn't do it himself...he already knew he was in trouble," Michael suggested.

"I wonder if he stole the book, realized what was inside, and then decided he was in way over his head." Ellie suggested.

"I think you're right," Michael said, "however, the only person that's going to know the answer—"

"Is his accomplice," Ellie said, completing Michael's thought.

"We've got to get to the Beach Comber Motel," Olivia stated, "before she skips town."

The trio pulled on their winter coats as they waited for George to finish his phone call. Ellie pressed the button on her fob to warm up her car.

"Are you guys heading out?" George inquired, surprised that everyone had their coats on.

"Yes," Michael replied, "we've got a lead that we want to chase down. Were you able to get in touch with Gordon?"

"Yes, yes, he's going to pick me up here. I mean," George smiled, somewhat embarrassed, "if it's okay that I stay here."

"Certainly, that's fine with me, make yourself at home." Michael paused in the doorway. "George, are you sure Drew didn't say anything about who you were supposed to give the book to?"

George hesitated, his gaze dropping to the floor. "No, Michael, I'm sorry. Just that it was someone at the Bernstein party."

Michael couldn't help but feel George was hiding something from them. He decided to push just a little more. "Yeah, almost impossible to figure out who. There was probably over a hundred people there."

"At least," George said.

"Did you see anything inside the book, or maybe initials on the cover, anything?"

"Nothing," George replied. "It was a black book with a leather cover, the size of an address book."

"We need to go, Michael," Ellie insisted, "we're running out of time."

Chapter 8

The Beach Comber Motel was located on the outskirts of Lana Cove festooned between a nearly empty strip mall and a mobile home lot. The motel had recently been painted a latte brown with white trim, making it look like the world's saddest gingerbread house. The rooms were tiny, rectangular boxes aligned in a row, each door decorated with a flimsy, plastic Christmas wreath with a plastic bow.

A neon-yellow oval sign sat balanced atop a blue-neon ocean wave. The oval sign was split into halves: the bottom was sandy brown and decorated with seashells, the top a brilliant blue. The words Beach Comber Motel beckoned to the discreet, and the bright neon-red vacancy let passersby know they were available to entertain their transgressions for only twenty-nine dollars a night.

Ellie eased her car into the motel lot and pulled in between a Jeep and a pickup truck, the back filled with snow-covered firewood.

Three police cars, lights flashing, were parked in front of the motel. The door to room number seventeen was open, and a uniformed officer watched them warily as they exited Ellie's car.

"That's not a good sign," Ellie said under her breath.

"Olivia, Ellie," Michael whispered, grabbing Ellie by the sleeve of her jacket. "That blue Honda." He tilted his head. "That's Drew's car."

"Oh no." Ellie shook her head, worried about the safety of the woman. "I should have called the police—"

Suddenly, a man burst out the door of room seventeen, his hands cuffed behind his back, followed by two police officers.

"I already told you! I heard yelling, the door was open, I just wanted to make sure she was okay! How was I supposed to know it was the television? I'm a hero."

"That's the guy from the pictures," Olivia said. "Tony, the electrician."

"Livs, there's Ryan." Ellie pointed at one of the officers escorting Tony to the back of the squad car.

"Ask my wife, she'll tell you!" Tony shouted. "I was only trying to straighten things out." He nodded toward a red-haired woman, bundled in a blue winter coat, an angry expression on her face.

"Yeesh, that guy might be safer in jail," Michael joked quietly.

"I think you're right," Olivia said. "That's one angry woman."

"Ryan," Ellie called out, waving to him.

The officer looked up, stared for a moment, and then his face relaxed when he recognized her. He spoke to his partner—Ellie imagined he was telling him that he knew her—and then he walked over. "Ellie, what are you doing here?"

"Helping Mr. West here do a little sleuthing," Ellie said, arching an eyebrow. "Ryan, this is

Michael West, future bestselling author, but mostly just unemployed."

Ryan gave Michael the once-over and then reached out and shook his hand.

"And you know Livs," Ellie said.

"Yes, of course. Hi, Olivia." Ryan gave her an awkward smile and an even more awkward wave, which Michael could tell he immediately regretted.

"Is she okay? The woman, is she okay?" Ellie asked before Ryan could ask her any more questions.

"Luckily, she wasn't here, but we did find this guy going through her stuff. Claims she—"

"Detective Mitchell," the other police officer called out, motioning him over.

"Just a minute," Ryan said, rolling his eyes. "Let me go see what Baxter needs. I'll be right back."

"One quick question," Ellie said. "Why is he after the woman who was staying here?"

"Long story short, he claims that he came here to confront her. Said she came on to him at a bar. Said they shared a couple drinks, the woman gave him a hug and left. Unfortunately for him, a couple of his wife's friends were at the bar and snapped some pictures of him with the woman. He said he brought his wife here to prove nothing happened."

"And he heard screaming inside," Ellie added, "so he burst into the room to make sure she was okay?"

"Yeah." Ryan nodded. "The television was really loud; I'll give him that. We got an anonymous tip that an assault was in progress, so we hightailed it over here and found this gentleman in her room. I'm sorry, I gotta see what Officer Jackson needs."

"Sure, sure, thank you, Ryan."

"So," Olivia asked as Ryan walked away, "do you think Tony's telling the truth?"

"My gut tells me yes," Ellie replied, "and I think Ryan's does, too. Who would bring their wife over here to confront another woman if he was going to do something…insane? I'm going to talk to his wife. You two wait here, I think she'll be more receptive if it's just one person and not three."

"Fair enough. Come on, Michael." Olivia motioned toward Ellie's car. "I think we've just been relegated to the children's table."

"Fine." Michael sniffed defiantly, a devious twinkle in his eyes. "Don't be surprised if we have this entire case solved by time you get back."

Ellie disappeared inside the motel's office and returned a minute later with a hot cup of coffee. "Heck of a night," she said to the woman. "Here's a cup of coffee."

"Thank you."

Ellie guessed the woman was about forty, her eyes tired, her cheeks and nose red from the cold. She cradled the cup for a moment, blew across the surface, and took a sip.

"Horrible night." She shook her head. "And who are you? Are you with the police department? You seem familiar."

"No, ma'am, I'm Ellie Banks. I own the Bitter Sweet Café."

"That's right." The woman smiled wanly. "Delicious coffee, and a lovely atmosphere. My name's Rita. So—"

"Yes," Ellie explained, "you're wondering why I'm, well, we," she gestured to Michael and Olivia, "are here."

The woman tilted her head and raised her eyebrows, as if to say: Well, tell me.

"We were driving down Ridgewood, and we saw the police cars. I recognized my friend over there," she pointed at Officer Ryan, "he's the guy talking on his phone, and, well, my curiosity got the better of me, so I stopped to see what was going on."

"Yeah, seems like curiosity got ahold of my husband, too, who's over there, the guy in handcuffs." She glanced at him and shook her head. "I've been married to him for twenty years—this Tuesday is our twenty-first anniversary—and this is what I get. My husband gawking at some spring chicken. And then to make matters worse, he gets arrested breaking into her motel room."

"I'm so sorry…but why would he be barging into a woman's motel room?"

"It's nothing," the woman said bitterly. She sipped her drink and waved as if shooing away the conversation.

Ellie took a gulp of her coffee and stared out at the parking lot, giving the woman her space.

"Ah, what the heck…. Tony's a good guy," she started. "He's smart, but he doesn't have any common sense. He admitted to buying the tramp a couple of beers and giving her a hug, but he said that was as far as it went, and I believe him. I'm mad because she stole his wallet. She went to the restroom and never returned, and when he went to pay his tab, he realized his wallet was missing. He put two and two together, ran out into the parking lot, just in time to see her jump into a blue car with Florida plates and speed off. That's the car," she said, pointing at the blue Honda.

"How the heck did you two ever find her?"

"It took almost a day and a half. He figured she was from out of town because of the Florida plates. So, he mapped off Lana Cove, and we have been to every bed and breakfast, hotel and motel in Lana Cove."

"And you decided to come with him?"

"After you get texts and photos from your friends that your husband is buying another woman drinks, and then your husband declares he's going to search all of Lana Cove until he finds her…." Rita's eyes filled with tears. "I love my Tony, but I don't like being made a fool of, and because of his stupidity, he'll probably lose a huge contract at the Bono estate."

"Wait, how would he lose his job? I'm sure Mr. Bono would understand that you had to take care of a few things since your husband's wallet was stolen."

"I wish it were that simple," Rita explained. "I couldn't care less about the woman. It's just that, we really needed this contract. The Bonos have a very strict security protocol for employees. Tony's been working for six weeks to get approved to work at their estate. He's been through background checks, his company has been investigated, and they even ran a background check on me. He was supposed to begin work today."

"I guess I'm just being dense," Ellie said, "but if your husband passed the background check, and they verified the legitimacy of his business...."

"The problem is, what was in his wallet. My husband was given a super-encrypted, all-access key card to the Bono estate. To put it simply, you do not lose this card. Now they would have to reissue cards for all of their staff and recode their alarm systems. That's the reason this is all so heartbreaking. This was a high-paying job and also a tremendous opportunity for Tony to make a name for himself and to land higher-paying clientele. Now, it's all over."

Ellie put her hand on Rita's shoulder. "Listen, Officer Ryan is a good guy. I've known him since high school. I'll do what I can for you and your husband, maybe they'll find that wallet, and he won't have to make that call…."

"Thank you so much. Tony's a good guy, too, he's never been in trouble."

Ellie handed Rita her phone. "Type in your number, and I'll let you know what I find out. I'll do whatever I can do, I promise you."

The woman nodded and closed her eyes, tears streaming down her cheeks. "Thank you," she whispered quietly as Ellie walked away.

Chapter 9

"So nice of you to return, Ellie. I'll have you know that in your absence, we busted the case wide open," Michael exclaimed.

"Really?"

Michael nodded and then shook his head. "Nope, we've got nothing. We know it's not George—"

"I can almost guarantee it's not this guy," Ellie said. "His wife's been playing *Where's Waldo* with him for the past thirty-six hours."

"I saw you speaking with Tony's wife." Officer Ryan joined the group. "Want to compare stories?"

"Sure, Rita said that her husband met Jane Doe at a bar, that he'd bought her a couple drinks, she went in for a hug—and relieved him of his wallet. He realized his wallet was missing when he went to pay his tab, and she claims that they've spent most of the past thirty-six hours scouring Lana Cove for her car."

Ryan nodded. "Did she say anything about how he got into the room?"

"She didn't mention that. She *did* mention that he'd just landed a very important contracting job at the Bono estate, and the wallet had his new security card in there. I have a feeling that it was more about getting that card back than anything."

"The Bono compound is like a fortress," Ryan concurred. "Losing that security card definitely isn't going to bode well for Tony."

"What's going to happen to him?"

"We'll bring him and his wife in for questioning—at this point he's looking at criminal trespass—but we'll see what the captain says."

"Did you find his wallet?" Michael asked.

"We did." Ryan nodded. "The credit cards, cash, and security card were gone."

"You didn't happen to find a little black book, did you, like an address book?" Ellie asked.

Officer Ryan closed his notebook and narrowed his eyes. "Ellie Banks, what aren't you telling me?"

Ellie kicked herself. "You know George, George Owens?"

"Yes, and if you know of his whereabouts, Ellie, he is a suspect in a homicide investigation."

"George showed up at Michael's house...."

Ryan's mouth tightened into a thin line.

"Ryan, this was before we knew anything had happened."

"Where is George now?"

"After we found out Drew had been killed, and George was a suspect, we told him he needed to turn himself over to the police. He called Gordon Sparks, his lawyer. They were on their way to the Lana Cove police department."

Ryan sighed. Ellie could tell he was upset with her, and rightfully so.

"What did George tell you?" he asked.

"He said Drew called him and told him to meet him at the Schooners restaurant if he wanted his job back. He said he needed him to do a favor for him, that he would explain the details in person."

"We have numerous witness accounts," Ryan confirmed, "that placed George at Schooners with Drew. Did he say anything else?"

"He told George he had a black book and he needed him to give it to someone at the Bernstein party. According to George, Drew acted like it was life or death. It frightened George so much that he refused."

"Did he say who he was supposed to give the book to?"

"No. But George did say that Drew kept looking around nervously. He even tried to force George to take the book, but when he wouldn't, George said Drew slammed him into the wall and took off running outside."

Ellie reached into her pocket and handed Ryan the memory card. "He said Drew dropped it when he slipped and fell on ice running to his car."

"Any idea what's on it?" Ryan asked.

"It's basically filled with photos of people Drew was blackmailing, pictures from the art expo, people's homes…a virtual who's who connecting Drew to a huge web of crimes."

"George gave you this card?"

"Yes, when he showed up at Michael's. He found it when he was walking to his car, on the ground where Drew slipped."

"Hmm." Ryan pulled out a baggie and placed the memory card inside. "Ellie, you said George told you he would get his job back if he delivered the book to someone at the Bernstein party?"

"That's right. George told me and my friends that it wasn't until he left the Bernsteins, and stopped for coffee at Waverly's, that he found out Drew had been killed. He saw the report on the news, saw Drew in his front yard, panicked, and drove straight to Michael's house."

"I just want to say," Michael spoke up, "that my house is not a safe haven for individuals wanted by the police. Please continue, Ellie."

Ryan's jaw tightened. "Ellie, George didn't work the Bernstein party. My family went to it—and the Santa that they had definitely wasn't George."

"What?" Ellie gasped. "But he told us…. Why would he lie to us?"

Officer Ryan fished his cell phone out of his pocket and punched in a series of numbers.

Michael, Ellie, and Olivia stood breathlessly waiting.

"Miller, it's Detective Mitchell. Has George Owens been processed?"

The sound came of fingers flying across a keyboard. "No, sir, it's a quiet night."

"Thanks, Miller. If he arrives, let me know ASAP."

"Yes, sir."

Ryan looked at the group and rubbed his head. "Seems like George is in the wind. Do me a favor, Ellie, let me know immediately if you see him, he could be dangerous."

Ellie wanted to vomit. How had everything turned out so wrong?

Chapter 10

Numb, Ellie climbed into her freezing car with Michael and Olivia. She took her phone from her pocket and dialed George's number. It went straight to voicemail.

"Ellie, we need to get back to my house. We need to find out if George is still there," Michael said.

"He lied to us…why would George lie to us?"

"He's afraid, Ellie," Michael said, touching her shoulder. "He's not thinking straight."

Ellie started the engine and pressed the front and rear defrost buttons. She put the car in reverse. The tires made a crunching sound in the snow. On the display from her rear backup camera she could see Rita, hunched over, her head in her hands.

"Ellie, maybe we should try calling George's lawyer…what was his name? Gordon something," Olivia said.

"Gordon Sparks," Ellie replied, turning onto Ridgewood.

"I'll check." Michael pulled up Google on his phone and searched for Gordon Sparks Esquire. "Found him." He tapped the speaker button.

The phone rang several times and then went to voicemail.

"Great." Michael sighed. "I'll leave a message. Hopefully he checks his voicemails."

"Wait," Olivia cried, "he's giving an emergency number."

Michael opened his notepad app and quickly typed in the number. "Got it."

Olivia met Ellie's eyes in the rearview mirror. This was hard on both of them. George was a close friend, and now he'd lied to them and may have killed a man.

"Hello." Michael's voice cut through the silence. He tapped the speaker button again and turned up the volume. "I'm Michael West, I'm a good friend of George Owens. I'm so sorry for the late hour, I wouldn't call if this wasn't urgent."

"Hello, Michael, what's this about?"

"I'm not sure if you've seen the news, but a man was killed in George's front yard."

"Yes, I tried phoning him a couple hours ago to make sure everything was okay, but it went straight to voicemail."

Michael looked at Ellie. She veered off the road into a Wawa gas station.

"So, George hasn't tried contacting you?" Michael asked.

"No, not this evening. Is everything okay?" Concern grew in the man's voice. "I'm guessing not."

"George came to my house when he found out Drew…was murdered. He told me he was worried about the police suspecting that he was to blame."

"Why on earth would he think such a thing?"

"George got into a fight with Drew at the Schooners bar, and a couple hours later, Drew wound up dead in his front yard. I told George to call you immediately. He faked a phone call to you and told me that you and he were going to the police station to clear all of this up. Now, no one can get ahold of him."

"Good Lord. What in the Sam Hill is he thinking?"

"I don't know. I'll give you a call if I hear anything. I'd greatly appreciate it if you would do the same. Everyone is terribly worried about him."

"I will. I take it the number you're on is your cell number."

"Yes, sir."

"Okay, I'll be in touch if I hear anything. Have a good evening."

"Goodnight." Michael hung up and turned toward Ellie.

Olivia leaned forward from the back between the two front seats.

"I need some coffee and some fresh air," Ellie exclaimed, pushing her car door open.

"I second that," Olivia said.

Michael hurried around the front of the car and joined the girls. "Listen, I have a theory. So far just about everything George has told us over the past twelve hours has been a lie."

Ellie gave him a harsh look.

Michael threw up his hands. "I'm sorry, Ellie, but it's true. Bernstein's party, calling his lawyer—"

"Okay, okay, so what's your point? I refuse to believe that George killed someone. I've known him my entire life. People don't just change."

"He snapped at the mall," Michael said. "Remember the entire beard incident? The truth is, we never know what will set someone off."

A bell tinkled as Ellie pushed open the door to the service station. She blinked at the harsh fluorescent overhead lights washing over them. Michael and Olivia followed at her heels and made a beeline to the back of the store, to the coffee counter.

"Hazelnut's fresh," a short, balding guy yelled out. He pointed at various pots of coffee. "French vanilla is fresh, and the pecan blend. The rest was made about three hours ago."

"Thank you," Olivia shouted back.

"So," Michael continued, pouring himself a large cup of hazelnut. "Remember when George said

Drew kept trying to force the book on him, and he wouldn't take it? What if Drew made him take it? What if Drew told George who the black book belonged to, and George tried to return it?"

"What do you mean, he tried to return it? What would stop him from giving someone a book at the Bernstein party?" Olivia asked.

"Unless," Ellie said suddenly, "he couldn't get in!"

"He couldn't get in? You think he showed up at their door and the Bernsteins said no, go away?"

"I think he got to their guardhouse, and they stopped him from getting in. Come on," Ellie exclaimed.

Michael threw a ten on the counter on the way out the door. "Three large coffees," he called out to the bewildered clerk as the door shut behind them.

Ellie gunned the engine and whipped the car onto A1A.

"Want to clue us in on where we're going?" Michael asked.

"Lantern Drive," Ellie replied, turning onto Sandy Pond Lane.

Michael stared out the window. The houses grew from elegant homes, to modest mansions, to sprawling oceanfront mansions. Ellie made a left onto Lantern Drive and came to a stop on a stone driveway. A brick guardhouse stood outside a set of ornate iron gates. Ellie slowly drove up and stopped at the gates.

A young man stepped from the guardhouse, his expression polite but stern. "May I help you?"

"Yes, please. I'm Ellie Banks, owner of the Bitter Sweet Café."

"Yes...?" he prompted.

"Look, this is embarrassing, but we are trying to locate a gentleman, who, let's say, is in a delicate mental state. His name is George Owens. He said that he was here, playing Santa."

The young man rolled his eyes. "He was here, but he was denied entrance. The Bernsteins have him on the no-admittance list."

"So, he wasn't allowed into the party this evening at all?"

"Nope. However, a few minutes later, Mr. Owens was apprehended when he tried to climb over the wall. We have security cameras mounted around the entire premises—not sure how he thought he was going to sneak in. I told him he was trespassing and I was going to call the police if he didn't leave immediately. Then he started going crazy, saying he had to deliver something to Giovanni Bono—he said it was life or death. The guy was scaring me. I radioed to my partner to call the police, and he bolted."

"Wait, Giovanni Bono, was he at the party?"

"I'm sorry, ma'am, but I can't tell you. That attendee list is kept private."

"One more question, sorry." Michael smiled, leaning across the front seat toward Ellie's window. "Do you have any idea what time that was?"

"Just a moment." The man sighed, disappearing into the guardhouse. He returned a moment later with a clipboard. "He arrived at eight-oh-seven p.m."

"Thank you so much, you've been a big help," Ellie said.

"Your very welcome, ma'am. Good luck." He instructed Ellie to reverse and then retreated into his guardhouse.

"Where to now?" Ellie asked, winding through the neighborhoods back to A1A.

Michael looked from Ellie to Olivia. "I think we all know where George is heading."

"Giovanni Bono's house," she said, the weight of impending doom crushing her.

"I think that black book is a lot more than just an address book," Michael said. "I know that Giovanni claims that his family ended their involvement with the Mafioso decades ago…but there are rumors that he is still very much entrenched in their operations. "Drew may have stolen a book that could implicate Giovanni in illegal activities—maybe not only Giovanni, but other powerful people," Michael continued. "They begin to close in on Drew, he panics and tries to get the book back to the Bonos but, he's seen too much."

"Which leaves George with the book," Ellie whispered. "He's going to take the book to the Bono estate." She hung her head. "George is as good as dead."

"Why wouldn't he just tell us?" Olivia asked. "We could have figured something out."

"Maybe he was going to," Ellie said, "but then he decided it was too dangerous—he probably didn't want anything to happen to us. So...?" she inquired.

"Lighthouse Lane," Michael replied, "the Bono house is on Lighthouse Lane. I think I'm going to do a Fodor's guide to criminal masterminds' estates when I've finished my mystery book," Michael revealed as they drove in silence. "Visit Sandpiper's Cove to visit Martin Peters's convicted serial killer estate. Next, residing in this charming Cape Cod, we have the home of Wilfred Moneybagger, known for crushing his victims under heavy bags of cash."

"Michael! Do you mind?" Ellie begged.

"Fine," Michael surrendered. "Turn right on Seaside, and then...," he glanced back at Google maps, "make a quick right on Lighthouse Lane."

"I don't think we should pull right up to his house," Olivia suggested. "The sign says it's a dead end. Maybe we should park a little further down the street."

"Good idea," Ellie said.

"It looks like his estate is a dead end, in more ways than one," Michael said, staring out the passenger-side window.

Ellie pulled her car along the curb. The Bono mansion was surrounded by a ten-foot stone wall that circled around the entire property, until it reached their private beach. A pier led from their deck, out to the ocean, where two speedboats were moored.

A cluster of spotlights and security cameras were mounted every fifteen feet, and the entrance was blocked by a massive wrought-iron gate.

The trio climbed out of Ellie's car and stood staring at the house.

"The Bonos and Bernsteins must shop at the same gate shop," Michael whispered.

"What now? It's not like we can just go up to the gate and ask them if they've seen George," Olivia reasoned.

"Why not?" Michael replied. "It worked pretty well at the Bernstein's. The only stupid question is the question not asked."

"Excuse me!"

They spun around, not expecting to hear a woman's voice behind them.

Michael clutched at his chest. "Good God, lady, you almost killed me." A small dog resembling a furry snowball sniffed Michael's shoe and then lifted its rear leg.

"Mildred McConey!" the woman gasped, reeling in her dog. "Mind your manners. I'm sorry about that."

"It's fine," Michael insisted, "I'm sure she was just stretching."

"Are you folks lost?" the young woman asked. She was dressed in snow boots, scrub pants, and a huge puffy white coat that made her appear as if someone had stuffed her inside a tower of powdered donuts. She brushed her hair away from her face with a gloved hand. "I wouldn't go snooping around the Bono's house if you know what I mean. Strange family." She tilted her head from side to side and rolled her eyes in a circle.

"We're trying to track down my grandfather," Ellie replied. "He's a professional Santa. You know, he does Christmas parties and events. The Bono house was the last one listed on his events calendar."

"He's getting old," Olivia added, "and we didn't see his car in the driveway. We're just worried about him."

"Does he drive a...." The woman scrunched up her face. "Actually, I don't know what kind of car it is—"

"A red car with wood paneling, a reindeer on the hood?" Ellie asked anxiously.

"Yes, that's it, you just missed them. A man drove by with a woman and another man who fits your grandfather's description, just a couple minutes ago."

"Thank you," Ellie exclaimed, already racing toward her car.

"Lighthouse Lane is one way," Michael said as Ellie spun the car around, spitting snow. "Seaside connects to A1A."

Ellie nodded, pouring on the gas. The car fishtailed and picked up speed. "If they're on A1A, we'll never catch them."

"If they go north," Michael said, "they'll be heading back toward town—"

"So?" Olivia asked.

"Town means more police, and since George is currently wanted by the police—"

"And his car stands out like a sore thumb," Ellie added and slid to a stop at the intersection of Seaside and A1A. "They're not going to want to go that way." She revved the engine and moved out onto the empty highway.

"Ellie, taillights," Michael blurted.

"I see them, I see them."

The taillights disappeared as the car pulled into a cove.

"That's the Atlantic Pier…this isn't good." Michael shook his head.

Ellie flicked off her headlights and eased her car behind a dumpster. "There's George's car," she pointed.

Michael was already nodding that he'd seen it.

Quietly, the trio exited the car, running low behind the dumpster. In the distance, three silhouettes walked toward the end of the pier.

"It's George, and Drew's friend. He's going to kill them," Ellie whispered, putting her hand over her mouth.

"We need to get to that shed," Michael said. "It's where they keep rental rods and equipment. If we can sneak up behind him, we might have a chance."

"A chance to do what?"

"I'm not sure," Michael replied, "I'm formulating a plan as I go, it's fluid."

"God help us," Ellie moaned.

Ellie, Michael, and Olivia crept through the darkness onto the pier. Below them, the waves crashed onto the shore, and above them, dark clouds raced across the sky.

A man dressed in black pants and a black hoodie gave the woman a vicious shove. "Keep moving," he snarled.

"Okay," Michael whispered, crouching behind the equipment shed. "Ellie, call the police. I'm going to do something stupid!"

"That's your plan? Michael!" She reached out to grab his arm, but it was too late, he was on the move.

The roar of the ocean covered the sound of Michael's approach. The wind whipped across the pier. He froze in his tracks.

The hooded man thrust his hand into his pocket and handed George something. "Turn on your cell phone," he demanded. "Hurry." He snatched the phone from George and launched it out into the ocean. "You look confused, old man," he mocked him. "You see, your cell phone will ping the closest tower, so after you kill her and push her into the ocean...the police will know that you were here. Plus, the red fiber from your suit on the pole over there...it's all the evidence the police are going to need."

The man put his gun to George's head. "You're going to shoot her. I'm going to let you live and take the rap for her death."

"I'll never shoot her!" George cried out.

"If you don't shoot her," the man spat, "I'll shoot her, and then I'll shoot you. Either way, she's going to die."

The woman flung her head from side to side. She tried to scream, but to no avail. Tape stretched across her mouth, blood caked around the edges, and terror glinted in her eyes.

The man roughly maneuvered George in front and placed a gun in George's hands. "That's right," he hissed, "now, I'm gonna help you kill her." He raised George's hands so the gun was level with her chest. "Good, now, all you've got to do is pull the trigger, and it will be over."

In the distance, a speedboat appeared, making its way across the ocean, heading toward the pier. The man turned his head for just a second, and that was when Michael slammed him in the back with a boat oar.

It all happened in an instant. The man toppled forward. George fired the gun, striking the woman in the leg. Horror flared in her eyes as she toppled backward off the pier into the ocean. Without a thought, George dived after her, into the churning, freezing ocean.

The hooded man whirled on Michael, his eyes filled with rage. In his hand, he held a gleaming knife with a serrated edge, shark teeth, for tearing and ripping flesh.

"You're an idiot." The man smiled. "And now you're dead."

"Actually," Michael said, "you've got your tenses wrong. I'm still alive. It should be: and now you're going to die."

The man's smile turned into a sickening sneer. He pivoted, twisting his body, and then hurled the knife at Michael's torso. There was a sickening thud. Michael stumbled backward, teetering on the edge of the pier. *This is it.* He waited for the searing agony, for that painful last beat of his heart.

"Michael!"

Ellie's scream tore through the night, and that was when Michael realized he had somehow blocked the knife with his oar. The man in the hoodie charged, and in the blink of an eye, Michael faked high and then brought the edge of the oar crashing into the man's knee.

He screamed in pain and fell to the ground, clutching his leg. Ellie rushed in, and Michael tossed the oar to her. Without hesitation, she smacked him in the back of the head, knocking him unconscious.

Olivia raced to the edge of the pier, scanning the water for George and the woman. Sirens wailed.

"There!" Ellie yelled, joining her.

George emerged from the water, stumbling to the shoreline, carrying the woman in his arms. A series of flashlights bobbed on the beach, heading toward George.

The black speedboat spun around in a tight U, throwing up a wall of water, and disappeared along the coastline, into the night.

Chapter 11

"And here we go, Ellie, a café latte with a dash of cinnamon," Michael said, putting a steaming cup in front of her.

"Are you sure the coffee's good here? You know I am a bit of a coffee snob."

"Oh…," Michael snatched a napkin from the table and folded it across his arm. "My lady, here at the Bitter Sweet Café we serve only the finest brews. We source our beans from local farmers in Costa Rica and Brazil. I'm sure that you will find your coffee pleasing to the palate."

"Bravo! Bravo!" Olivia laughed. "You're hired."

Michael gave a slight bow. "Lady Olivia, you look magnificently stunning this morning. I bring to you a caramel macchiato with freshly whipped cream."

"Gorgeous," Olivia whispered.

"Thank you," Michael replied. "I get that a lot. And, Sir George the Brave, a cup of our finest joe with a splash of cream and two squares of sugar."

"Thank you, Michael." George beamed up at him. "Masterfully done."

"Thank you." Michael flung the napkin from his arm with a flourish. "I shall return momentarily."

"I think someone finally got some sleep." George chuckled.

"I think so. It's been a stressful few days for everyone." Ellie smiled.

"Did I miss anything?" Michael asked, sliding into his seat and sitting two cups of coffee on the table.

"Two cups, Michael?" Olivia stared at him, shaking her head.

"I couldn't decide. There was pumpkin spice and then cookies and cinnamon. I'm going to alternate sips. I believe William Cowper said it best, in his famous poem *The Task*. Variety is the very spice of life, that gives it all its flavor."

"Well, if it's in a poem," Ellie reasoned, "then it has to be true."

"Undeniably," Michael agreed.

"So, George," Ellie said. "I spoke to Officer Ryan. He said that you're free and clear."

"Yes, thank you so much, Ellie." George nodded. "And thanks, you guys, too." He smiled at Olivia and Michael. "If it hadn't been for your help, things would have ended much differently. I'm terribly sorry for lying to all of you.... Michael, I came to your house and wanted to tell you all the truth about the book—when I went to your bedroom to call Gordon and ask him what to do, my phone rang. It was Sarah. She told me they were going to kill her if I didn't bring the book to the Bonos." He shook his head. "I knew that I just couldn't get you all involved. So I decided to continue hiding the book and lied about calling Gordon."

"It's okay, we understand," Ellie said, giving George a compassionate smile. "I would have done the same thing."

Michael and Olivia nodded in agreement.

"Did you see what was in the book?" Michael asked.

"No, Sarah tried to tell me, but I told her I didn't want to know. She told me Drew stole it to try to get back into the good graces of the Calvetti crime family—but of course, it didn't work out that way."

"Do you think the police are going to investigate Mr. Bono? I hear his family has been untouchable for generations," Ellie asked.

"I don't know." George shook his head and clasped his weathered hands on the table. "Detective Mitchell thinks Mr. Bono will be well insulated from anything that happens. He said they found his car. There were bloodstains in the trunk that were a match to Drew—the gun recovered at the pier was registered to him. There are multiple witnesses. The Bonos are saying they have no idea who the man at the pier was, and that he acted on his own. Plus, witnesses at the Bernstein's party claim that Mr. Bono was there during the entire party."

"So you never saw Mr. Bono?" Ellie asked.

"No, only the man who tried to kill us."

"What's going to happen to Sarah?"

"I don't know.... She knows what's inside the book. Maybe she'll exchange information for a lighter sentence—maybe even witness protection, who knows?"

Ellie nodded, deep in thought.

Michael looked at his friends and shook his head. "Come on, guys, why the mournful expressions? We stopped a murder, broke up a crime ring, and…," he pulled out three envelopes. "A little Christmas gift."

George gave Michael a curious stare.

"I'll explain later, but for now…," Michael handed each of his friends an envelope.

"Twelve hundred dollars," Olivia gushed. "Michael, this is too much."

"It's not from me," he exclaimed, "it's from our mystery friend. He gave us five thousand dollars, and I'm dividing it equally."

"I don't deserve this." George slid his envelope back across the table.

"You deserve it more than any of us," Ellie said. "You protected your friends; you risked your life to save Sarah—"

George's face turned bright red. "Thank you, Ellie."

Michael's eyes widened, and his heart sank. The local news had George's picture on the screen. The news anchorwoman stood on the pier, where just a few hours ago, George and his friends had battled for their lives.

Ellie glanced around the café warily. Everyone's attention was focused on the television. She wanted to jump from her seat and rip the cord from the wall, but she sat there, as if glued to her chair.

The anchorwoman's hair whipped around her face. She pulled up her collar on her coat to try to shield her microphone from the wind. "Police tell us that just a few hours ago, Gabriel Roccio was arrested after attempting to murder Sarah Lewis and George Owens. Sarah was shot in the leg, and George Owens dove off the end of the pier to rescue her."

The cameraman pointed the camera down into the crashing waves some forty feet below.

"We have some video of that rescue—we apologize for the quality." The screen went black as the video image moved up and down.

"Help him!"

The video swung up again, showing crashing waves, and then George, carrying a woman in his arms, the waves pounding at his back. He disappeared below the surface and then reemerged, fighting to keep the woman's head above the surface.

"Two other people raced into the water to help him. George struggled to the shore and collapsed. We can see cameraman's hands and feet in the video as he helps to pull George out of the water."

The words *Lana Cove Hero* scrawled across the screen.

The Bitter Sweet Café was silent for a moment, the only sound was the drumbeat of *The Little Drummer Boy* and the news anchor saying Sarah Lewis was hospitalized.

All of a sudden, a man leaped to his feet and shouted, "George, George!" throwing his fist into the air.

Soon the entire café was on their feet shouting, "George!"

Michael studied Ellie. She was beautiful, her brown eyes filled with joy. He pulled a card from his pocket and slid it across the table to her.

"What's this?" she asked. The outside of the card read: *Inside this card lies your secret desire.* "Oh, well, I'm not sure I want to look at this here."

"Go on," Olivia exclaimed.

Ellie rolled her eyes and opened the envelope. A spring-loaded mistletoe branch shot up, hovering over her head.

She gazed at Michael and smiled. "Okay, you win."

"Yes!" Michael stood and leaned across the table, puckering his lips.

Ellie stared deep into his eyes and then turned and gave George a kiss on the cheek. "Merry Christmas, George."

George's face turned bright red, and his nose glowed like Rudolph's. Michael's mouth fell open as he glanced from Ellie to George, then back to Ellie.

"Maybe next year." Olivia laughed, patting him on his back.

George looked adoringly at his friends and winked at Michael. "Best Christmas ever, best Christmas ever."

More from T. Lockhaven

We hope you enjoyed reading *Sleighed*, the first book in *The Coffee House Sleuths: A Christmas Cozy Mystery* series.

The characters and location in *Sleighed* are a part of *The Coffee House Sleuths* series. If you enjoyed Sleighed, then join Michael, Ellie and Olivia in *A Garden to Die For*, available at Amazon and Barnes & Noble.

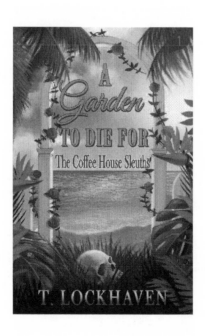

Also a children's author under the name Thomas Lockhaven, you may find his other works on our website: twistedkeypublishing.com

Ava & Carol Detective Agency Series

Book 1: The Mystery of the Pharaoh's Diamonds

Book 2: The Mystery of Solomon's Ring

Book 3: The Haunted Mansion

Book 4: Dognapped

Book 5: The Eye of God

Book 6: The Crown Jewels Mystery

Book 7: The Curse of the Red Devil (Upcoming title)

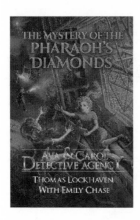 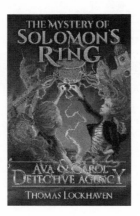 

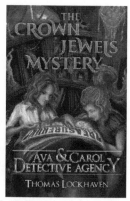

The Ghosts of Ian Stanley Series

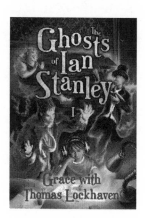

Quest Chasers Series

Book 1: The Deadly Cavern
Book 2: The Screaming Mummy

If you enjoyed the book, please leave a review on Amazon, Goodreads, or Barnes & Noble. We'd love to hear from you! Thank you so much for reading our book, we are incredibly grateful!

Learn about new book releases by signing up at the website twistedkeypublishing.com.

Made in the USA
Middletown, DE
05 November 2021

51742649R00092